I0726349

SPIRITS OF THE BORDER:

THE GHOSTS OF ALBUQUERQUE

BY

KEN & SHARON HUDNALL

THE GHOSTS OF ALBUQUERQUE

COPYRIGHT © 2017 KEN HUDNALL

All rights reserved. No part of this book may be reproduced or transmitted in any form or by any means, graphic, electronic, or mechanical, including photocopying, recording, taping or by any information storage or retrieval system, without the permission in writing from the publisher.

OMEGA PRESS

An imprint of Omega Communications Group, Inc.

For information contact:

Omega Press

5823 N. Mesa, #839

El Paso, Texas 79912

Or http://www.kenhudnall.com

FIRST EDITION

Printed in the United States of America

OTHER WORKS BY THE SAME AUTHOR
FROM OMEGA PRESS

KEN AND SHARON HUDNALL

MANHATTAN CONSPIRACY SERIES
Blood on the Apple
Capitol Crimes
Angel of Death
Confrontation

THE OCCULT CONNECTION
UFOs, Secret Societies and Ancient Gods
The Hidden Race
Flying Saucers
UFOs and the Supernatural
UFOs and Secret Societies
UFOs and Ancient Gods
Evidence of Alien Contact
Sensual Alien Encounters
Secrets of Dulce
Intervention

SHADOW WARS
Shadow Rulers
Underground America

DARKNESS
When Darkness Falls
Fear The Darkness

SPIRITS OF THE BORDER
(with Connie Wang)
The History and Mystery of El Paso Del Norte
The History and Mystery of Fort Bliss, Texas

(with Sharon Hudnall)
The History and Mystery of the Rio Grande
The history and Mystery of New Mexico
The History and Mystery of the Lone Star State
The History and Mystery of Arizona
The History bnd Mystery of Tombstone, AZ
The History and Mystery of Colorado
Echoes of the Past
El Paso: A City of Secrets

Tales From The Nightshift
The History and Mystery of Sin City
The History and Mystery of Concordia
Military Ghosts
Restless Spirits
School Spirits
The History and Mystery of San Elizario, Texas

THE ESTATE SALE MURDERS
Dead Man's Diary

OTHER WORKS

Northwood Conspiracy

No Safe Haven; Homeland Insecurity

Where No Car Has Gone Before

Seventy Years and No Losses:

The History of the Sun Bowl

How Not To Get Published

Vampires, Werewolves and Things
That Go Bump In The Night

Even Paranoids Have Enemies

Criminal Law for Laymen

Understanding Business Law

Language of the Law

Border Escapades of Billy the Kid

PUBLISHED BY PAJA BOOKS
The Occult Connection: Unidentified Flying Objects

DEDICATION

As with all of my books, I could not have completed this book if not for the support and assistance of my lovely wife, Sharon.

TABLE OF CONTENTS

CHAPTER ONE
THE LAND OF ENCHANTMENT

New Mexico has long been called a timeless land of ancient cultural traditions and striking environmental diversity. It has also been called a land where the unusual is sometimes taken for granted.

For thousands of years, man has traveled through this unusually beautiful land leaving footprints to a rich and colorful past. Some of the earliest known inhabitants included the Paleo-Indians of the Folsom Period who wandered into the area hunting the animals upon which their very survival depended. Animals that have now been extinct for more than 10,000 years.

The earliest settlers of this land of mystery are believed to be tribes of Indians that farmed the fertile land along the Rio Grande, producing corn, beans and squash. One of these early civilizations that settled in this region was the mysterious race that is today called the Anasazi. We do not know what this early civilization called itself, as the word "Anasazi" is a Navajo word meaning "Ancient Ones." They are thought to be ancestors of the modern Pueblo Indians, inhabited the Four Corners country of southern Utah, southwestern Colorado, northwestern New Mexico, and northern Arizona from about A.D. 200 to A.D. 1300, leaving a heavy accumulation of house remains and debris.

Recent research has traced the Anasazi to the "archaic" peoples who practiced a wandering, hunting, and food-gathering life-style from about 6000 B.C. until some of them began to develop into the distinctive Anasazi culture in the last millennium B.C. During the last two centuries B.C., this historically wandering people began to supplement their food gathering with maize horticulture. By A.D. 1200 horticulture had assumed a significant role in the economy[1].

Because their culture changed continually (and not always gradually), researchers have divided the occupation into periods, each with its characteristic complex of settlement and artifact styles. Since 1927 the most widely accepted nomenclature has been the "Pecos Classification," which is generally applicable to the whole Anasazi Southwest. Although originally intended to represent a series of developmental stages, rather than periods, the Pecos Classification has come to be used as a period sequence:

- Basketmaker I: pre-1000 B.C. (an obsolete synonym for Archaic)
- Basketmaker II: c. 1000 B.C. to A.D. 450
- Basketmaker III: c. A.D. 450 to 750
- Pueblo I: c. A.D. 750 to 900
- Pueblo II: c. A.D. 900 to 1150
- Pueblo III: c. A.D. 1150 to 1300
- Pueblo IV: c. A.D. 1300 to 1600

---

[1] This research was conducted by Nicole Torres and Steven Stuart and reported at http://www.crystalinks.com/anasazi.html

- Pueblo V: c. A.D. 1600 to present (historic Pueblo)

The last two periods are not important to this discussion, as the Pueblo peoples had left Utah by the end of the Pueblo III period.

As the Anasazi settled into their village/farming lifestyle, recognizable regional variants or subcultures emerged, which can be usefully combined into two larger groups. The eastern branches of the Anasazi culture include the Mesa Verde Anasazi of southeastern Utah and southwestern Colorado, and the Chaco Anasazi of northwestern New Mexico. The western Anasazi include the Kayenta Anasazi of northeastern Arizona and the Virgin Anasazi of southwestern Utah and northwestern Arizona. To the north of the Anasazi peoples - north of the Colorado and Escalante rivers - Utah was the home of a heterogeneous group of small-village dwellers known collectively as the Fremont.

Although they continued to move around in pursuit of seasonally available foods, the earliest Anasazi concentrated increasing amounts of effort on the growing of crops and the storage of surpluses. They made exquisite baskets and sandals, for which reason they have come to be known as "Basketmakers."

They stored their goods (and often their dead) in deep pits and circular cists - small pits often lined with upright stone slabs and roofed over with a platform of poles, twigs, grass, slabs or rocks, and mud. Basketmaker II houses were somewhat sturdier than those of their archaic predecessors, being rather like a Paiute winter wickiup or a Navajo Hogan. Very few have been excavated.

By A.D. 500 the early Anasazi peoples had settled into the well-developed farming village cultural stage that we know as Basketmaker III.

Although they probably practiced some seasonal traveling and continued to make considerable use of wild resources, they primarily had become farmers living in small villages.

Their houses were well-constructed pit structures, consisting of a hogan-like superstructure built over a knee-or waist-deep pit, often with a small second room or antechamber on the south or southeast side.

Settlements of this time period are scattered widely over the canyons and mesas of southern Utah; they consist of small hamlets of one to three houses and occasionally villages of a dozen or more structures.

By about A.D. 700 evidence of the development of politico-religious mechanisms of village organization and integration appears in the form of large, communal pit structures. One such structure, with a diameter of forty feet, has been excavated next to the old highway in Recapture Creek by archaeologists from Brigham Young University.

Three important changes took place before A.D. 750: the old atlatl (spear thrower) that had been used to propel darts (small spears) from time immemorial was replaced by the bow and arrow; the bean was added to corn and squash to form a major supplement to the diet; and the people began to make pottery. By A.D. 600 the Anasazi were producing quantities of two types of pottery - gray utility ware and black-on-white painted ware.

By A.D. 750 these farming and pottery-making people in their stable villages were on the threshold of the lifestyle that we think of as being typically Puebloan, and from this time on we call them Pueblos.

Perhaps the most significant developments in Pueblo I times (A.D. 750 to 900) were:

- the replacement of pit house habitations with large living rooms on the surface
- 2) the development of a sophisticated ventilator-deflector system for ventilating pit rooms
- 3) the growth of the San Juan red ware pottery complex (red-on-orange, then black-on-orange, pottery manufactured in southeastern Utah)
- 4) some major shifts in settlement distribution, with populations concentrating in certain areas while abandoning others.

The two-hundred-fifty-year period subsequent to A.D. 900 is known as Pueblo II. The tendency toward aggregation evidenced in Pueblo I sites reversed itself in this period, as the people dispersed themselves widely over the land in thousands of small stone houses.

During Pueblo II, good stone masonry replaced the pole-and-adobe architecture of Pueblo I, the surface rooms became year-round habitations, and the pit houses (now completely subterranean) probably assumed the largely ceremonial role of the pueblo kiva. It was during this period that small cliff granaries became popular.

The house style known as the unit pueblo, which had its beginning during the previous period, became the universal settlement form during this period. In the unit pueblo the main house is a block of rectangular living and storage rooms located on the surface immediately north or northwest of an underground kiva; immediately southeast of this is a trash and ash dump or midden.

The red ware pottery industry continued to flourish, as a fine, red-slipped ware with black designs was traded throughout much of the

Colorado Plateau. During the middle-to-late Pueblo II period, however, the red ware tradition ended in the country north of the San Juan River, although it blossomed in the area south of the river.

Virtually all of the red or orange pottery found in San Juan County sites postdating A.D. 1000 was made south of the San Juan River around Navajo Mountain in the Kayenta Anasazi country. The reasons for this shift are unknown, and the problem is a fascinating one. Production and refinement of the black-on-white and the gray (now decorated by indented corrugation) wares continued uninterrupted in both areas, but the red ware tradition migrated across what appears to have been an ethnic boundary.

The styles of stone artifacts also changed somewhat during Pueblo II. The beautiful barbed and tanged "Christmas tree" style point that had been popular since late Basketmaker III times was replaced first by a corner-notched style with flaring stem and rounded base, then by a triangular style with side notches.

Also, by the end of the period, the old trough-shaped metate that had been popular for half a millennium was replaced by a flat slab form with no raised sides. The change in grinding technology appears to have accompanied a change from a hard, shattering, flint type of corn to a soft, non-shattering flour corn. This permitted use of smaller metates, and thus also increased the efficient use of the floor space.

During the 1100s and 1200s the Anasazi population began once again to aggregate into large villages. This period is known as Pueblo III, and it lasted until the final abandonment of the Four Corners country by the Anasazi during the late 1200s. Numerous small unit pueblos continued to be occupied during this period, but there was a tendency for them to become more massive and to enclose the kivas within the room block.

A number of very large villages developed. It was during this period that most of the cliff villages such as the famous examples at Mesa Verde National Park and Navajo National Monument were built.

During Pueblo III times the Mesa Verde Anasazi developed the thick-walled, highly polished, incredibly beautiful pottery known as Mesa Verde Black-on-White.

They also continued to make corrugated gray pottery. Red wares, often with two- or three-color designs continued to be imported north of the river from the Kayenta country. Arrowheads continued in the triangular, side-notched form, but were often smaller than those of the previous period.

Starting sometime after A.D. 1250 the Anasazi moved out of San Juan County, often walking away from their settlements as though they intended to return in a few minutes - or so it looks. Why did they leave behind their beautiful cooking pots and baskets? Perhaps because they had no means to transport them. When forced to migrate a long distance, it was more efficient to leave the bulky items and replace them after they reached their destination.

We do know that they moved south. Classic late Mesa Verde-style settlements can still be recognized in New Mexico and Arizona, in high, defensible locations in areas where the local Anasazi sites look quite different. By A.D. 1400 almost all the Anasazi from throughout the Southwest had aggregated into large pueblos scattered through the drainages of the Little Colorado and Rio Grande rivers in Arizona and New Mexico. Their descendants are still there in the few surviving pueblos.

By the end of the 13th century, the Anasazi had completely abandoned their high-walled cities in northwestern New Mexico and the rest of the Four Corners area and drifted south where, along with the farmers from the Rio Grande, they developed the sophisticated Pueblo communities.

Shortly before the arrival of the Spanish, the Athapascan tribes entered the Southwest. Divided into two related groups, the Apache and the Navajo, the Athapascans established permanent villages only in the last 200 years.

SEVEN CITIES OF GOLD

In the 16th century, the Spaniards in New Spain (now Mexico) began to hear rumors of "Seven Cities of Gold" called "Cibola" located across the desert, hundreds of miles to the north[2]. The later Spanish tales were largely caused by reports given by the four shipwrecked survivors of the failed Narváez expedition, which included Álvar Núñez Cabeza de Vaca and an African slave named Esteban Dorantes, or Estevanico. Eventually returning to New Spain, the adventurers said they had heard stories from natives about cities with great and limitless riches. However, when conquistador Francisco Vázquez de Coronado finally arrived at Cibola in 1540, he discovered that the stories were unfounded and that there were in fact no treasures as the friar had described — only adobe towns.

While among the towns, Coronado heard an additional rumor from a native he called "the Turk" that there was a city with plenty of gold

---

[2] The stories may have their root in an earlier Portuguese legend about seven cities founded on the island of Antillia by a Catholic expedition in the 8th century.

called Quivira located on the other side of the great plains. However, when at last he reached this place (conjectured to be in modern Kansas, Nebraska or Missouri), he found little more than straw-thatched villages.

QUIVIRA

As Coronado arrived at the Rio Grande, he was disappointed by the lack of wealth among the Pueblos, but he heard from an Indian (whom the Spaniards called "the Turk") of a wealthy civilization named "Quivira" far to the east, where the chief supposedly drank from golden cups hanging from the trees. Hearing of this, Coronado led his army of more than one thousand Spaniards and Indian aides onto the Great Plains in 1541. The Turk was his guide to Quivira.

THE CORONADO EXPEDITION - 1540–1542

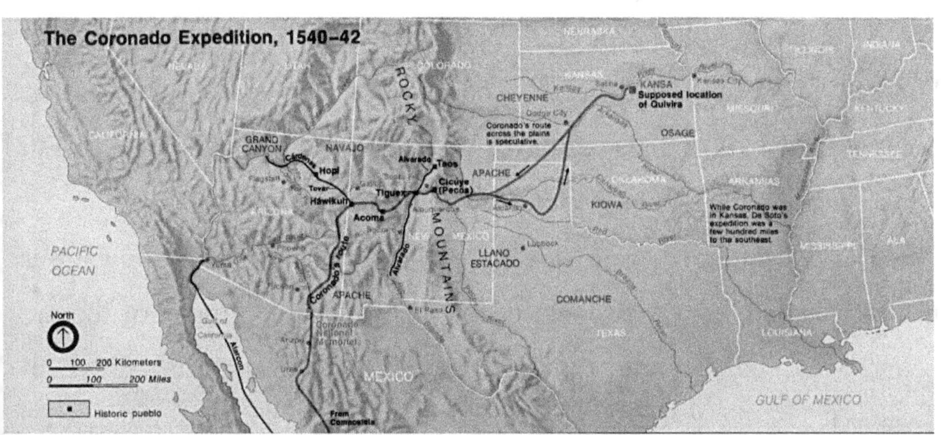

Figure 1: The Route of Coronado's 1540 Expedition

On his journey, Coronado traversed the panhandle of Texas. He found two groups of Indians, the Querechos and the Teyas. He was heading southeast when the Teyas told him that the Turk was taking him the wrong direction and that Quivira was to the north. It appears the Turk was luring the Spaniards away from New Mexico with tales of wealth in Quivira, hoping perhaps that they would get lost in the vastness of the Plains. Coronado sent most of his slow-moving army back to New Mexico. With 30 mounted Spaniards, priests, Indian followers, the Turk, and Teya guides he had forced into service, he changed course northward in search of Quivira. After a march of more than thirty days, he found a large river, probably the Arkansas, and soon met several Indians hunting buffalo. They led him to Quivira.

Coronado found Quivira "well settled...The land itself being very fat and black and being very well watered by the rivulets and springs and rivers. I found prunes like those of Spain, and nuts and very good sweet grapes and mulberries." It was, he said, the best land he had seen during his long trek north from Mexico. Coronado spent 25 days in Quivira and traveled about 65 miles (25 leagues) from one end of the country to the other. He found nothing more than straw-thatched villages of up to two hundred houses each and fields of corn, beans, and squash. He found no gold, other than a single small piece which he reasoned had come into the natives' hands from a member of his own expedition.

The Quivirans were simple people. Both men and women were nearly naked. They "were large people of good build" many of the men being over six feet tall. They seemed like giants compared to the Spaniards.

Coronado was escorted to a farther boundary of Quivira, an area called "Tabas," where the neighboring land of Harahey began. He summoned the "Lord of Harahey" who, with two hundred followers, came to meet the Spanish. The Harahey Indians were "all naked—with bows and some sort of things on their heads, and their privy parts slightly covered. It was the same sort of place... and of about the same size as Quivira."

Disappointed at his failure to find wealth, Coronado turned his face toward New Mexico and marched back across the plains, met up with the rest of his army there, and the following year returned to Mexico. Before leaving Quivira, Coronado ordered the Turk strangled. The Coronado expedition had failed in its quest for gold.

Coronado left behind in New Mexico several Catholic priests and their helpers, including Friar Juan de Padilla. Padilla journeyed back to Quivira with a Portuguese assistant and several Christian Indians. The friar and most of his companions were soon killed by the Quivirans, apparently because he wished to leave their country to visit their enemies, the Guas. The Portuguese and one Indian survived to tell the story.

Vasquez de Coronado trekked throughout much of New Mexico in 1540, in search of this vast treasure. He became convinced that the adobe pueblos he found were in fact the legendary Seven Cities of Cibola[3]. Coronado had orders to conquer the Indians and claim their riches.

---

[3] The **Seven Cities of Cibola, were** legendary cities of splendor and riches sought in the 16th century by Spanish conquistadores in North America. The fabulous cities were first reported by Álvar Núñez Cabeza de Vaca who, after being shipwrecked off Florida in 1528, had wandered through what later became Texas and northern Mexico before his rescue in 1536. The viceroy of New Spain, Antonio de Mendoza, sent an expedition in 1539 under Estéban, a black slave who had been shipwrecked with Cabeza de Vaca, and Fray Marcos de Niza to verify de Vaca's reports. Fray Marcos, assured of the cities' existence by an Indian informant, claimed to have seen them in the distance. In 1540 Mendoza dispatched Francisco Vázquez de Coronado to search for the cities. Instead of finding the legendary cities, though, Coronado encountered only Indian settlements—including the Zuni Pueblos, which originally had inspired the false legend—even though he explored as far north as modern Kansas.

Conquering the Indians he met was not a great problem but the riches he sought were still far out of reach.

It should be noted that The Seven Cities of Gold is a myth that led to several expeditions by adventurers such as conquistadors in the 16th century. It is also featured in several works of popular culture. According to legend, the seven cities of gold could be found throughout the pueblos of the New Mexico Territory. The cities were Hawikuh, Halona, Matsaki, Kiakima, and Kwakina. While there have always been mentions of a seventh city, no evidence of a site has been found. After failing to find the fabled golden cities, however, Coronado and his men returned to New Spain without any newly won wealth.

Don Juan de Oñate made the first successful exploration of Mexico del Norte's wilderness. In 1598 he marched up the Rio Grande claiming land for Spain, accompanied by troops, colonists and cattle.

Santa Fe was founded as the capital in 1609 by New Mexico's third governor, Don Pedro de Peralta. For the next 70 years the Spanish pushed on with sword and cross, building missions and converting Indians to Catholicism whether they wanted to be converted or not.

The first church in North America was constructed in 1598 at San Juan Pueblo, 30 miles north of Santa Fe. Within the first quarter of the 17th century, 50 churches had been built in New Mexico. These churches, which predate the great missions along the coast of California by a century and a half, are beautiful examples of Spanish Colonial architecture and provide a glimpse of the earliest history of American culture.

Some Indians accepted Christianity, others found it oppressive. By the middle of the 17th century, there was growing discontent among the Pueblo people. On Aug. 10, 1680, after years of careful planning, the tribes rose up and drove the Spanish out of Santa Fe in the great Pueblo Revolt. By 1692, however, the Spanish had returned. Don Diego De Vargas, the newly appointed governor and captain-general of New Mexico, began to reconquer the northern pueblos, a task that took four years.

New Mexico remained under Spanish rule for another 125 years until 1821 when Mexico won its independence from Spain. Soon after, another passage in New Mexico history was born, the Santa Fe Trail. Running from Missouri to Santa Fe, the trail opened trade with the U.S. and brought new lifestyles, money and settlers to New Mexico.

The United States declared war on Mexico in 1846. Shortly thereafter, U.S. General Stephen Watts Kearny maneuvered his troops down the Santa Fe Trail and declared New Mexico an American territory

During the U.S. Civil War, federal troops, aided by the New Mexico Volunteers, foiled a Confederate invasion at Apache Pass near present-day Glorietta.

Figure 2: Billy the Kid and his brother Joseph

In the late 1880s, railroad companies laid their tracks across New Mexico, bringing with them improved commerce and access to new markets. The beef industry boomed, and cattle barons like John Chisum trailed longhorns in from Texas, creating vast cattle kingdoms on the southeastern plains.

Chisum was also associated with events leading to the Lincoln County War, a bloody merchant conflict that sparked the brief outlaw career of Billy the Kid and involved even territorial Gov. Lew Wallace, author of the novel Ben-Hur.

Although New Mexico was colonized nearly 25 years before the Pilgrims' arrival at Plymouth Rock, it did not achieve statehood until Jan. 6, 1912, when it was admitted to the Union as the 47th state. Since that time, New Mexico has experienced a whirlwind of growth and change.

Two regiments from New Mexico endured the Bataan Death March during World War II, while Navajo "code talkers" used their native language to send military messages that were incomprehensible to the Japanese. On July 16, 1945, the first atomic bomb was detonated at Trinity Site near Alamogordo, a dramatic opening to the nuclear age.

In the decades between 1940 and 1980, New Mexico's population tripled. The state now boasts more than a million and a half inhabitants, a third of whom live in Albuquerque, New Mexico's largest city.

Centuries-old agricultural and ranching traditions exist alongside a rapidly developing electronics industry. Los Alamos National Laboratory and Sandia National Laboratory in Albuquerque are leaders in the defense industry, taking giant steps forward in energy-related and high-tech computer research.

UNDERGROUND ALIEN BASES?

Certainly no book on New Mexico would be complete without at least touching on all of the many stories about secret underground alien bases that are supposed to be hidden around the state.

Buried deep in the desert near Dulce, New Mexico are caverns allegedly populated by aliens. Numerous abductees have reported being taken to the base to be examined, and most have seen members of various branches of our military, primarily USAF personnel interacting with these mysterious aliens. According to some reports, the aliens are carrying on genetic experimentations, in secret agreement with our government.

In 1969, according to ex-Naval Intelligence Officer Milton Cooper, a confrontation took place between the aliens and our own scientist in which 60 humans were killed. This site is said to be connected to the installations at Los Alamos by an underground shuttle.

However, let me stress that the U.S. government, especially the USAF, denies any knowledge of any alien base, joint genetic experiments, or any deaths of either civilian and/or military personnel connected to this non-existent base.

CHAPTER TWO
LOST TREASURES IN NEW MEXICO

Like the Spanish did in every region that they conquered, they searched for treasures, both of nature and of man. The search for the fabled wealth of this mysterious new land was inevitable. Coronado's quest of these treasures and lost cities led to the eventual discovery, exploration, and the naming of New Mexico. Although the Franciscan friars that were accompanying each exploration effort were searching for new converts, the rest of the exploration parties were really searching for the wealth that might be in the region of New Mexico.

Francisco Vasquez de Coronado was an ambitious adventurer who desired great wealth. He searched for fabled cities with vast treasure, but these places were not to be found. Instead, his quest for increased wealth left him with huge financial losses and a tarnished reputation.

Coronado was the governor of Nueva Galicia when Fray Marcos de Niza returned from Cibola. He heard Fray Marcos' tales of seeing one of the seven cities and went with him to meet with Viceroy Antonio de Mendoza. Mendoza selected Coronado to lead the expedition which was funded by themselves and other investors.

As they crossed southeastern Arizona, supplies began to run out. After six months on the trail, the ragged expedition entered Cibola for rest and food supplies. Many future expeditions into New Mexico would also arrive low on provisions and would continue the trend of expecting the Indians to supply their needs. Leaving Cibola in pursuit of riches, they entered Hawikuh and the group immediately saw that Fray Marcos' stories were lies. A detachment under Pedro de Tovar was sent to Tusayan in northern Arizona, but this village inhabited by the Hopi Indians was in poor condition too. Another group, led by Captain Garcia Lopez de Cardenas, went west and found the Grand Canyon. Melchor Diaz located the lower Colorado River and then crossed into the desert area of California.

An Indian chief named Bigotes led them to a new province called Tiguex where Tiwa pueblos were built next to the Rio Grande River. Coronado, needing shelter for his army, made the Indians vacate the village of Alconfor. He then ordered the Tiwa villagers to provide them with grain and blankets. The Indians rebelled and two villages were demolished by the Spanish. Coronado's diplomatic blunder set the pattern for other explorations for exploitation of the Indians and led to the growing mistrust of the Spanish by the Indian tribes.

While wintering in the village, an Indian named Turk told Coronado tales of riches in the east. The following spring, the expedition left for the fabled Quivira, but they only discovered the grass houses of the Wichita Indians. Due to his apparent fabrications, Turk was killed by Spaniards frustrated by the failure of their expedition.

By the expedition's completion, Coronado suffered from financial loss and a broken spirit. Charges were brought against him alleging his abuse of the Tiguex Indians and his failure to enlarge Spanish holdings by not establishing a settlement near the Rio Grande River. Coronado was acquitted on these charges, but his reputation was ruined.

This expedition was a success in other ways. The adventure expanded the world's geographical knowledge of North America. His men were the first Europeans to see the Grand Canyon and the Colorado River, to explore the pueblo interior, to reach the Continental Divide, to associate with the Hopi Indians, and to cross the plains of North America. Historically, he is remembered more for these successes then he is for his failure to find the seven lost cities.

The three sub-expeditions that were off-shoots of Coronado's "Big Search" were attempts by the leader to locate hidden wealth that might be in the Southwest. After Coronado failed to find any riches in New Mexico, he sent smaller groups from the expedition in other directions. Every time a new story or rumor was told by local and visiting Indians, he sent his troops in search of the fabled city or treasure. Sub-expeditions were sent westward with the hope that something was out there to be found. Garcia Lopez de Cardenas discovered the Grand Canyon of Colorado. Pedro de Tovar encountered the Hopi Villages. Melchor Diaz located the Colorado River and searched into the desert region of California. Each sub-expedition returned without any financial success.

Coronado is an important historical figure because of his travels and the discoveries of his sub-expeditions. Although none of the sub-expeditions found any wealth, they are historically important because these sub-adventures expanded the world's geographical knowledge of North America.

The Spanish attitude toward the Indians was that they saw themselves as guardians of the Indian's basic rights. The Spanish goal was for the peaceful submission of the Indians. The laws of Spain controlled the conduct of soldiers during wars, even when the tribes were hostile. The missionary's role was to convert the Indians to Christianity. This would be followed by the Indians being accepted as members of the Spanish civilization. However, the exploitation of the Indian occurred constantly.

The Anglo attitude was one of total removal from their lands or total inhalation. The Indian was continually pushed aside or killed.

The colonial Spaniards put great faith in the legends and myths which were being told throughout Spain. These beliefs led Fernando Cortez to discover Mexico. Spanish soldiers conquered the Aztec Indians, and discovered precious metals. Astonishing tales concerning great treasures in the North were being told by local and visiting Indians.

The Spanish, believing the tales of the Indians, began searching for the Seven Cities of Gold, the Gran Quivira, the Seven Cities of the Seven Bishops, and the Seven Caves of Origin of the Aztecs. During 1536, four survivors of the Narvaez Expedition arrived in Culiacan. Alvar Nunez Cabeza de Vaca claimed to have seen only small supplies of cotton shawls, beads, and turquoise among the Indians during his trip. He also saw five arrowheads made out of emeralds. However, he reported hearing stories of people who lived in large houses in the North who traded in turquoise and other goods.

In 1539, a Spanish Franciscan friar named Father Marcos de Niza set out with friendly Indians and Estevanico, the black slave from the Narvaez Expedition party, to learn the secrets of the North. When the friar returned to Mexico City from the journey he falsely claimed to have seen one of the fabled cities from a distance. The friar's news led to the expedition of Francisco Vasquez de Coronado. Coronado's expedition and all other Spanish expeditions to follow were centered around the search for the fabled riches and lost cities.

The search for the fabled wealth was inevitable. Coronado's quest of these treasures and lost cities led to the eventual discovery, exploration, and the naming of New Mexico. Although the Franciscan friars were searching for new converts, the rest of the exploration parties were really searching for the wealth that might be in the region of New Mexico.

Francisco Vasquez de Coronado was an ambitious adventurer who desired great wealth. He searched for fabled cities with vast treasure, but these places were not to be found. Instead, his quest for increased wealth left him with huge financial losses and a tarnished reputation.

Coronado was the governor of Nueva Galicia when Fray Marcos de Niza returned from Cibola. He heard Fray Marcos' tales of seeing one of the seven cities and went with him to meet with Viceroy Antonio de Mendoza. Mendoza selected Coronado to lead the expedition which was funded by themselves and other investors.

As they crossed southeastern Arizona, supplies began to run out. After six months on the trail, the ragged expedition entered Cibola for rest and food supplies. Many future expeditions into New Mexico would also arrive low on provisions and would continue the trend of expecting the Indians to supply their needs. Leaving Cibola in pursuit of riches, they entered Hawikuh and the group immediately saw that Fray Marcos' stories were lies. A detachment under Pedro de Tovar was sent to Tusayan in northern Arizona, but this village inhabited by the Hopi Indians was in poor condition too. Another group, led by Captain Garcia Lopez de

Cardenas, went west and found the Grand Canyon. Melchor Diaz located the lower Colorado River and then crossed into the desert area of California.

An Indian chief named Bigotes led them to a new province called Tiguex where Tiwa pueblos were built next to the Rio Grande River. Coronado, needing shelter for his army, made the Indians vacate the village of Alconfor. He then ordered the Tiwa villagers to provide them with grain and blankets. The Indians rebelled and two villages were demolished by the Spanish. Coronado's diplomatic blunder set the pattern for other explorations for exploitation of the Indians and led to the growing mistrust of the Spanish by the Indian tribes.

While wintering in the village, an Indian named Turk told Coronado tales of riches in the east. The following spring, the expedition left for the fabled Quivira, but they only discovered the grass houses of the Wichita Indians. As reported earlier, due to his fabrications, the Indian known as the Turk was killed by Spaniards frustrated by the failure of their expedition.

Though a failure by many standards, this expedition was a success in other ways. The adventure expanded the world's geographical knowledge of North America. Coronado's men were the first Europeans to see the Grand Canyon and the Colorado River, to explore the pueblo interior, to reach the Continental Divide, to associate with the Hopi Indians, and to cross the plains of North America. Historically, he is remembered more for these successes then he is for his failure to find the seven lost cities.

THE LOST DUTCHMAN MINE

One of the most famous lost treasures in the state of New Mexico is called the Lost Dutchman Mine. For over a hundred years, men have searched for this supposed vast hidden treasure. Searching had died down for a time until the finding of the mysterious Peralta Stones.

Figure 3: Stone Heart

About once a year someone discovers the Peralta Stones and immediately jumps to the conclusion that they have at long last found the key to the whereabouts of the Lost Dutchman Gold Mine. And without further ado, not even a flake of gold, or any serious research, they immediately want to tell everybody about it. I hope no one is taking all of this too seriously and investing a lot of time and money in any scheme to recover the Dutchman's treasure based on the clues in these stone tablets. Many believe that there are no legitimate clues there.

The Peralta Stones are a set of engraved stones that some people believe they indicate the location of the famed Lost Dutchman's Gold Mine, in Arizona, United States[4]. The stones are named for the Peralta family, said to be an old and powerful Mexican family. Peralta is a common Hispanic surname. Some people named Peralta owned a cattle ranch that included what is now Oakland, California at the time of the Mexican–American War. Pedro de Peralta was the governor of the Spanish territory in New Mexico, and picked the site for Santa Fe.

James Reavis popularized the idea of a rich Peralta family in Arizona in 1882, when he tried to assert the phony Peralta Spanish land grant, which included a huge swath of Arizona and New Mexico, including the Superstition Mountains; Reavis' forged Peralta genealogy was exposed, and he served a prison sentence for fraud. According to current legend, but not supported by the historical record, some Peraltas mined in the Superstition Mountains.

The first written reference to a "Peralta mine" in the Superstitions was in 1895, by writer Pierpont C. Bicknell. The stones consist of "two red sandstone tablets and a heart-shaped rock made of red quartzite. Each block is approximately 8.25" by 14" and 2" thick, weighing about 25 lbs. Each red stone block is carved with lines and one long line. When the two blocks are placed side by side and the stone heart is inserted the long line has 18 dots pecked into it. This style of map is known as a Post Road Map

---

[4] The Dutchman was a German immigrant named Jacob Waltz.

and it is a style used in Mexico and Spain during the Mexican–American War. Inscribed on the stones is the date 1847, and one stone contains a relief of a heart, which the heart-shaped stone fits perfectly. The heart shape fits neatly in the second stone. The back of the stone that the heart-shaped stone fits into has the outline of a cross carved on the back. The back of the other stone has the word DON carved into it.

There is confusion about the discovery of the Peralta Stones. Some say they were found by a man named "Jack" in 1956 (one source says 1952, another 1949) near the main highway that goes from Apache Junction, Arizona, in the vicinity of Black Point (33°16'19.86"N by 111°19'38.36"W). Another item found at this site is known as the Latin Heart.

The two red sandstone map pieces are displayed with a third white sandstone of similar size and weight as the red ones. The history of the white stone was cited by an author using the moniker 'Azmula'. Azmula cites the history in the Superstition Mountain Journal, issue 27 of 2009. He attributes the original citation to M. Kraig Roberts. Mr. Roberts's article is titled "History of the Chain Of Possession Of The Stone Maps". The Journal article is a history of the white stone. The white sandstone has a side showing a Priest who is assembling the Peralta Stones to form the map. The reverse side is known as the Horse Map. The Priests Stone contains Spanish text that states that to find the gold you must find the heart. The lower half of the number 8 in the red sandstone map has a small heart carved in the circle.[5]

---

[5]Kesselring, Robert and Lynda (2013). Reading Peralta Maps :Volume 1, Maps of Stone and Skin (1st ed.). LuLu.com: LuLu Publishing Services. pp. 53–58. ISBN 9781483405339

The story of the Peralta Stones' discovery and the stones themselves are not very convincing to most researchers. The engravings appear to have been created using modern power tools, with modern symbols, and modern Spanish.

Father Charles Polzer, an ethno historian associated with the Arizona State Museum, is convinced the stones are fakes. Among other reasons, he says that the modern valentine-shaped symbol used to denote a heart was a symbol unknown to 19th-century Spaniards.

The stone tablets are now in possession of the Arizona Museum of Mines and Minerals in Phoenix. They're not on display, but the folks at the museum will be happy to show them to anyone who is interested. They'll also be happy to tell you what they know about them, which is plenty.

A number of people have alleged that they have compared the drawings on the stones to topographical maps of various places in the Superstition Mountains and found them to coincide with the terrain.

Many people have been convinced of the authenticity of the Peralta Stones because the Peralta family name is mentioned so often in the history books. It's true that the Peraltas were many and that some of them were quite prominent in business and in politics in their time. Don Pedro de Peralta was installed in 1609 as the first governor of the Spanish Territory of New Mexico. The territory actually had a more elaborate Spanish name suggesting a kingdom, and it included almost the whole southwestern quarter of the United States, but it's usually referred to as the Spanish territory.

Don Pedro was so far from Spain that he did pretty much as he pleased in the name of the king, and he appointed his relatives to all of the important government posts in the territory. He also had the power to make land grants in the name of the king, and he did so for several of his friends and relatives. One of the largest Spanish land grants in the New World was the famous Peralta holding in California, which was held intact until the late 19th century by Don Luis Peralta and his heirs.

Peraltas multiplied at an astonishing rate in the New Mexico territory, as well as in Chihuahua and Sonora. Peralta became a common family name, and there were thousands of them by the middle of the 19th century. Today Peralta is still a common surname in Mexico and the U.S. Southwest. The Phoenix telephone directory lists dozens, and every city in California and New Mexico has its fair share of Peraltas.

So who are these particular Peraltas who figure so prominently in the Lost Dutchman legend? The two blamed most often are Pablo Peralta and his youngest son, Miguel.

Pablo Peralta owned a silver mine in Ures, Sonora, for many years, but by the middle of the 19th century the silver was about exhausted and corruption in the local government forced him to abandon the mine. He moved his family to the Mother Lode country in Central California. There is substantial documentary evidence of their presence in Tuolumne County during the Gold Rush years.

It was probably about 1863 when Pablo and Miguel left California and went to Arizona. They held a registered mining claim on the Agua Fria River a few miles from present day Black Canyon City, and they called their mine the Valenciana, the same name as the abandoned silver mine in Mexico. The existence and location of that mine is well documented, and prospectors today occasionally rework the tailings that the Peraltas left behind.

In all probability, the Valenciana produced a fair amount of gold, but Indian raids were always a problem, and Pablo and Miguel were attacked several times. During one of the battles an Indian with a lance seriously wounded Pablo. Miguel then sold the mine to a group of investors from California, and they moved to the new town of Wickenburg, about a hundred miles to the southwest, which was booming after the discovery of the Vulture mine.

Shortly after they arrived in Wickenburg, Pablo died of his wounds. Miguel then opened a dry goods store, married, and prospered. He opened a second store in Seymour when the Central Arizona Mining Company constructed its stamp mill there in 1879. Later on, he moved to Phoenix where he opened a larger general merchandise store at the corner of Washington Street and Center Street – now Central Avenue – the geographical center of the modern Phoenix.

Although there were several authentic Spanish land grants in what is now the State of Arizona, none of them involved anyone with the surname Peralta. However, there is reason to believe that Miguel was involved with Doc Willing and James Addison Reavis in the infamous Peralta-Reavis Spanish Land Grant affair, which was a complete fabrication and a fraud. Doctor Willing died of natural causes in 1872 before the fraud was discovered; James Addison Reavis ultimately went to prison for his part in the scheme, and Miguel fled to Mexico. He later took his own life in a Nogales, Sonora, hotel room. But that's another story.

All of this, of course, does not preclude the possibility that some of the other Peraltas may have mined gold and/or silver in the Superstition Mountains during some period of time. There is evidence of early Spanish and Mexican mining activity in the general area, and it's reasonable to assume that some of the Peraltas would have had a hand in it, given their numbers and the prominence of the family.

Getting back to the Peralta Stones, one writer states that Professor Dana, a geologist at the University of Redlands in California, examined the stones and issued a letter attesting to the fact that they were more than one hundred years old. If such a letter ever existed, no one admits to having seen it or knows what may have happened to it.

The University of Redlands was founded as a liberal arts college in 1907. The university has since covered a broad field of studies over the years and currently offers more than forty majors in thirty departments. Professor Dana is not presently on the faculty.

There have been a number of published comments in Desert Magazine since the stories about the Peralta Stones were published, and many of them serve to confuse the issue even more. One writer wrote that the father of a friend had been the Arizona State Mine Inspector during the time Jacob Waltz was alive, and he contended that Jacob Waltz's gold looked like it was high-graded from the Vulture mine.

When Jacob Waltz died in 1891, Arizona was a territory; statehood did not come until 1912. The territorial government registered claims and protected property rights, after a fashion, but it did nothing else to control the mining industry. There was no Mine Inspector in Jacob Waltz's time. The first mine inspector in Arizona was appointed in 1912; however, he didn't actually get around to inspecting any mines until late in 1913. Jacob Waltz had been in the ground more than twenty years and the only gold samples known to have been in his possession had disappeared on the day he was buried.

It is, of course, possible for a trained individual to determine with a reasonable amount of certainty what mine or mining district a particular ore sample came from, but the process is more involved than just looking at an ore sample. One chunk of ore looks pretty much like all other chunks of ore to the naked eye. However, there are many people who still believe that Jacob Waltz's gold was stolen from the Vulture mine. I don't believe it for the simple reason that every merchant in Wickenburg was buying high-graded Vulture gold directly from miners in those years. Certainly they knew that the gold was stolen from the mine, but there were no questions asked and no tales told. There was no reason for Jacob Waltz to travel all the way to Wickenburg to buy high-graded gold from the miners, and there is not one scrap of evidence that he did so.

There is evidence that Jacob Waltz went to Wickenburg with Jack Swilling and a group of German miners from the Weaver district in 1863. Swilling, an engineer, went there to build the Corbin mill on the Hassayampa River about eight or ten miles northeast of the Vulture mine. And there is also evidence that many of those who helped in the construction stayed on to work at the mill after it was finished. The Corbin Mill processed a considerable amount of ore from the Vulture, and Waltz would probably have had access to Vulture gold at that time. It is most likely, however, that he never actually worked at the Vulture mine.

It is equally probable that Jacob Waltz left Wickenburg when the Corbin mill closed and Swelling and his crew of German immigrants went to Phoenix to dig irrigation canals. The first canal was called the Dutch Ditch because so many of those involved in its digging were Germans, all of whom were offered quarter section homesteads when the ditch was completed. Jacob Waltz's homestead is well-documented, so we can assume that he was one of the ditch diggers. All of this is speculation, of course, but it seems to me to be reasonable speculation, much more so than the stories that have him living in Phoenix and running back and forth to the Vulture mine to fence gold ore for the miners. Sixty miles was a long trip in those days.

Figure 4: Sample of Gold Ore in Possession of Waltz.

Jacob Waltz did have a lot of gold when he was living in Phoenix, and its source has never been satisfactorily explained. Let's keep in mind, though, that he was a prospector and a gold miner all of his life, and he was pretty good at it. The Southwest desert is full of gold; you just have to know where to look, how to recognize it when you find it, and how to get it out of the ground and into your pocket. None of that would have been much of a problem for Jacob Waltz.

PART II

HAUNTED ALBUQUERQUE

ALBUQUERQUE, NEW MEXICO

Figure 5: Don Francisco Cuervo y Valdez

Albuquerque, New Mexico's largest city was named to honor a Spanish Duke, the 10th Duke of Albuquerque. Colonial Governor Don Francisco Cuervo y Valdez selected the name but over the centuries, the first "r" has been dropped.

In 1706, Albuquerque was founded by a group of colonists who had been granted permission by King Philip of Spain to establish a new villa (city) on the banks of the Rio Grande (which means big or great river). The colonists chose a place along the river where it made a wide curve providing good irrigation for crops, a source of wood from the bosque (cottonwoods, willows and olive trees) and nearby mountains. The site also provided protection and trade with the Indians from the pueblos in the area.

Figure 6: Church in Old Town

The early Spanish settlers were religious people, and naturally, the first building erected was a small adobe chapel. Its plaza was surrounded by small adobe homes, clustered close together for mutual protection against any threats posed by hostile forces in this vast and dangerous country. The church, San Felipe de Neri, still stands on the spot. The building itself has been enlarged several times and remodeled, but its original thick adobe walls are still intact. The church is the hub of Old Town, the historic and sentimental heart of Albuquerque, with activity revolving around shopping and dining. To this day, special holidays and feast days are still commemorated as part of the year-round attractions of this "original" Albuquerque.

A Great deal of history was made in and around this historic old city. The area known as Old Town is well known as a place where the past meets the present in a unbelievably fascinating world of shops and a window into the past of this ancient city. Whether due to its age or its location, or simply the open mindedness of its citizens, but the City of Albuquerque is also well known as a place where ghosts walk the night and the past literally comes alive. Join us for a stroll through a number of haunted locations that we shall explore in this volume.

ALBUQUERQUE PRESS CLUB
201 Highland Park Circle, SW,
Albuquerque, NM 87102

Figure 7: The Albuquerque Press Club.

The Albuquerque Press Club is an organization that was founded in order to promote fellowship and understanding among men and women engaged in journalism and its allied fields. It also sponsors such cultural, educational and social activities as may promote good fellowship and professional growth among members; and to extend reciprocity to similar clubs in other parts of the nation and world. The Albuquerque Press Club is over a hundred years old at the time of this writing.

After a long search, the Albuquerque Press Club purchased the Whittlesey House in the seventies as its permanent quarters. This historic old home was designed by architect Charles F. Whittlesey and built on the Highland east of Albuquerque to be his family home in 1903[6]. It is a

---

[6] http://www.albuquerquepressclub.org.

three-story frame structure designed after a Norwegian villa. Low-pitch roofs with exposed log fronting, rough log-cut facades and a wide porch, which surrounds its eastern rooms, characterize the house.

In 1908 the Whittleseys sold the property to Theodore S. Woolsey, Jr., Assistant District Forest Ranger U.S.F.S, who owned the house for the next twelve years. Early photos suggest that he added the addition to the south side of the house and framed out the northwest corner of the main porch. Records show that in 1916 he leased the house to Mr. Andros, President of Whitney Hardware, and in 1917 to Mr. Raynolds, President of the First National Bank.

In 1920, Arthur Hall purchased the home from Theodore Woolsey for his new bride. In fact, according to the history of this historic old home, she refused to marry him unless he purchased this particular house as their home. Also, this was not to be a happy home for the couple, as Clifford Hall, the woman who would wed Arthur Hall only if this particular house was her home, divorced her husband in 1930. In the property settlement, she was adamant that she wanted ownership of the house that she had come to love. In fact, she lived in her house for the next forty years. It was 'home' to her more than to any family prior to or after her ownership. She brought the house through periods of extensive remodeling and interior style changes.

By 1935, the former Mrs. Hall was remarried to Herbert McCallum, but this too would end in divorce in 1938. During the periods of time that she was single, Clifford supplemented her regular income as a nurse by renting portions of the house. The south porch was framed out and part of the first level was sealed off to make a separate apartment The original stable was renovated and added to, making it into an apartment complex. An additional apartment was built adjacent to it. As new building materials were introduced, Clifford resurfaced the interior walls of the house. 'Whittlesey's rough wood and burlap surfaces were covered by celutex, plaster and wood planking.

Figure 8: Original Structure

Clifford McCallum loved this old home and put her heart and soul into making it into a showplace. However, there comes a time when the frailty of the human form becomes an added factor that must be considered. So too did this happen to the indomitable Clifford McCallum.

Though it was as hard as selling one of her children, in 1960 Clifford McCallum sold the house. Her increasing age, the extensive upkeep on the structure and numerous other reasons contributed to her decision. Zeta Mu Zeta House Corp. of Lambda Chi Alpha Fraternity purchased the house to be a fraternity house. The structure with it many rooms and apartment-like situation suited the fraternity well. Little information was available about the fraternity's activities, their members having moved elsewhere, inadequate fraternity records, etc. The fraternity sold the house in 1966 to John T. Roberson, who leased the structure.

<u>A BIT OF HISTORY ABOUT CHARLES F. WHITTLESEY</u>

Charles Frederick Whittlesey was born on March 10, 1867 in Alton, Illinois. He studied architecture in Chicago under Louis Sullivan, whose influences can be seen in Whittlesey's later concrete structures in California. The extent of friendship between Whittlesey and Frank Lloyd Wright, who also worked in Sullivan's office during this time period, is unknown. But, the expertise that Whittlesey was to later gain in reinforced concrete in California, prior to its extensive use by Wright, suggests that the two friends shared information when their paths again crossed in California.

In 1891 (age 24) Whittlesey began his own practice. Within this decade, he married his first wife, Edith May, and began to raise his family -- two sons, Harold and Austin and two daughters, Enid and Beatrice. He made his home in Riverside, a suburb of Chicago.

By 1900 (age 33) the Santa Fe Railroad, in recognizing Whittlesey's originality and talent, appointed him chief architect in charge of hotels and stations. Thus, in 1901 he came to Albuquerque, New Mexico to supervise the construction of the Alvarado Hotel. This hotel was one of his most noted works, with its mission style and pueblo Indian motif, characteristic of railroad structures extending to and through California. During these early years of the century, Whittlesey conducted his business from Albuquerque, as might be noted by a classified ad appearing in the Albuquerque Journal Democrat during the first half of May 1902:

"Architect, Charles F. Whittlesey, Main off. Albuquerque, Branch off. Chicago, El Paso, Los Angeles, Patronage solicited all over the southwest. Wide experience to all kinds of building."

Whittlesey's family arrived in Albuquerque on May 8, 1902, just three days prior to the opening of the Alvarado Hotel.

"Architect Whittlesey is happy for another reason besides the opening of the new hotel. His wife and children arrived yesterday from Coronado Beach."

The family residence, it seems, would always be a distance from Charles Whittlesey's active concerns. While the family resided in Albuquerque, 1902 to 1905 and possible as late as 1908, he was active supervising the construction of the well-known Harvey Hotels at Merced, Bakersfield, and Cochran, California; Trinidad, Colorado; Raton, New Mexico, and Shawnee. It was in 1902, in Albuquerque, that he designed tow structures in log and stone. The first of these was the El Tovar hotel at the Grand Canyon, a design still recognized today. The other was his Albuquerque residence, the structure covered by this survey.

By 1905 Charles Whittlesey was spending most of his time in Los Angeles. During these years, he observed, studied and tested the principles of reinforced concrete until he became convinced of its value as a building material. In Los Angeles, he designed and directed the construction of the Philharmonic Auditorium (1905) and soon afterwards, the Hunington Hotel in Pasadena (originally Hotel Wentworth). The Philharmonic

Auditorium was designed with cantilevered concrete balconies (max. cantilever 28' and concrete bowed beams (max. span 112').

The Hunington Hotel used cellular concrete construction consisting of 6" bearing walls at each room partition, continuous floor slabs and no furred ceiling space. For their day, they were hold and innovative uses of reinforced concrete.

In 1906 Whittlesey went to San Francisco to assist in its reconstruction after the earthquake. The Pacific Building (still standing today at 421 Market, the southwest corner of Market and 4th SL), a ten-story concrete structure, is an example of his work there. His expertise in reinforced concrete was well noted by 1908, both in the many buildings that bore his name and in the various writings and expositions he wrote.

The Whittlesey family followed Charles from Albuquerque to Los Angeles and San Francisco. They lived there through 1920. Charles conducted his practice from the Pacific Building through 1912 and then from his residence. In 1912 his first wife Edith divorced him. He later married Mabel. His son Austin studied under him and later became an architect; Harold became a structural engineer, both collaborating on many designs built on the West Coast. Of Whittlesey's life and work beyond this date, little information was available at the time of this writing.

For the record, the following four buildings designed by Whittlesey are listed:

In Los Angeles:

- The Mayflower Hotel (1926-27);
- The residence of Mrs. Bartlett;
- The Whittlesey Residence (corner of Pico Blvd. and St. Andrews Place (unknown if still existent); and

- The Green Hotel in Pasadena.

THE GHOSTS

It was no secret that Clifford Ball McCallum loved this house more than anything else in the world. So is it any wonder that even after her death that she would want to keep an eye on the house where she had spent so much of her life? The spirit of "Mrs. M", as she has become known, has been known to appear in the bar area. Some bartenders even go so far as to leave a drink on the bar in case she should want a drink.

The sound of high heeled shoes has been heard by several witnesses walking across the floors of the bar and lobby area. Noises have also been associated with the pool table in a room downstairs. Voices and balls moving about on the pool table of their own accord comprise a few of these accounts. The piano in the lobby has also been played (3 notes) by an unseen presence.

The apparition of a woman in a black shawl has been reported on several occasions in various locations throughout the building. Cats at the club have been observed watching and hissing at an unseen presence.

THE ARROYRO
Albuquerque, New Mexico

Figure 9: The Haunted Arroyo

The Arroyo is located near Winrock Shopping Center and believed to be haunted by Albuquerque's version of La Llorona. This particular spirit is called "el Yorone" the crier is the ghost of a mother whose child was drowned in the drainage ditch. It is said at night she wanders the ditch crying and searching for her lost child.

CARRIE TINGLY CHILDREN'S HOSPITAL
1113 University Boulevard
Albuquerque, New Mexico

Figure 10: Staff and Patients

Until the 1930s, a child with polio was most likely to be kept home and very little said. However, during the 1930s, Franklin Delano Roosevelt was elected President of the United States. President Roosevelt also suffered from Polio. Suddenly the disease was nothing to be hidden, but one to be fought with all of the assets at the disposal of the government. So it was that in the autumn of 1937, the doors opened on New Mexico's new children's hospital. This new facility was named after Carrie Tingley, wife of then Governor Clyde Tingley, who felt a hospital was needed for the children of the state who were suffering from polio.

Again following the example of President Roosevelt, the Tingleys chose the site of Hot Springs, later named Truth or Consequences, located in southern New Mexico. It was known for its healing mineral waters, and it resembled the site in Warm Springs, Georgia, where their friend President Franklin Roosevelt was treated for polio.

As polio became less widespread due to new vaccines, the hospital direction began to focus on other orthopedic conditions such as scoliosis, clubfoot, cerebral palsy and spina bifida.

In 1981, the hospital moved to Albuquerque to align itself closer with medical services and consultants here. In 1987 the UNM Board of Regents was appointed as the CTH Board of Directors. Subsequent legislative action merged Carrie Tingley Hospital with the UNM Medical Center.

Carrie Tingley Hospital is now a component of the University of New Mexico Health Sciences Center. CTH houses a 24-bed inpatient unit and conducts 21 specialized clinics for children from birth to 21 years of age. A community outreach program visits 16 communities throughout New Mexico, enabling rural patients to be seen by CTH doctors and staff.

Surgery is also performed at University Hospital. All children who are residents of New Mexico may receive services. Rehabilitation is in-house under the care of board-certified doctors and therapists. Carrie Tingley Hospital has a full service orthotics and prosthetics department to meet all the children's needs.

THE GHOSTS

Less well known are the stories of hauntings that have spread about the facility occupied by the hospital when it moved to Albuquerque.

It is said that there are some unused portions in the hospital building that contain glowing rooms and strange figures are seen to walk the halls.

Other former employees talk about invisible "force fields" that do not allow a person to pass into certain rooms. The force fields also make a static/hissing sound when encountered by an unsuspecting worker.

There have also been stories regarding voices being heard that cry out for help, no subsequent searches turn up no one who could have called for help. At other times sounds similar to very loud heartbeats can be heard echoing through the silent halls. Several witnesses maintain that they have seen black robed figures walking about the hallways, though again, subsequent searches reveal no robed figures.

DESERT SANDS MOTEL
5000 Central Avenue, SE
Albuquerque, New Mexico

Figure 11: Desert Sands Motel

The Desert Sands Motel was built in 1957 and is comprised of 67 rooms on two floors. Once described as a first class facility in the 1960s, this motel has certainly seen better days. As has happened to many formerly top notch motels, it is now living out its days as a resting place for drifters and those with little disposable income. The Desert Sands Motel is now ranked number 116 in a ranking of hotels/motels in

Albuquerque. On the other hand it is a cheap and easy place to stay when you're headed west on Interstate 40.

THE HAUNTINGS

Several guests who stayed in the corner room on the first floor of the center building have reported that they had some very unusual things happen to them. Several said that almost as soon as they had entered their room and put their bags down on the bed, unusual things began to happen. There were cold spots in some parts of the room and unexplainable voices were heard coming from the bathroom.

In addition to the mysterious voices, the water in the bathroom ran by itself and the TV in the room kept turning on and off on its own. As if this was not bad enough, when it was not turning itself off, the television set was also changing channels by itself. The final straw for these guests was when the outside door kept unlocking of its own accord.

HOTEL ANDALUZ
125 2nd St NW, Albuquerque

Figure 12: Lobby of Hotel Andaluz

It began as Conrad Hilton's fourth hotel in 1939, and in 2008, the Andaluz was completely restored to its original grandeur. The historic place is said to be haunted; the apparition of a woman in 1940s clothing has been seen in the hallways, and another ghost is that of an older woman in a pink dress that seems to reside on the fourth floor. Apparitions also appear in the second-floor ballroom. Late afternoon or evening is the most common time for them to appear.

Further research turned up the following confirmations regarding haunted experiences. Guests at the Hotel Andaluz have describe being woken by a puff of wind in the face, and having their jewelry moved while sleeping. The hotel's ghosts like to occupy the second, fourth and seventh floors as well as the ballroom.

No one has any theories on why the ghost of a young female partygoer still dressed in her 1940s best, searches for her room on the seventh floor of the Hotel Andaluz or if she has anything to do with another ghost — an elderly woman in a pink dress — who wanders the fourth floor. The only thing that's known is that the ladies have been haunting the place since 1939, when hotel magnate Conrad Hilton opened it as the Hotel Hilton. It's had many owners and many names over the course of its 60- year history.

"The hotel recently underwent a $30 million renovation and is now the Hotel Andaluz," according to hotel spokesperson Joanie Griffin. "The ghosts don't seem to care; they're still here no matter what it's called."

HAUNTED HILL
The end of Menaul
Albuquerque, New Mexico

Figure 13: Haunted Hill

The location called Haunted Hill is said to be located at the end of Menaul. This broad thoroughfare crosses the city of Albuquerque until it ends in the foothills.

Though who have ascended this haunted high ground report that they could hear the sounds of women screaming, footsteps crossing the hard packed earth and what sounded like bodies being drug through the dirt.

Others have reported seeing a lantern swinging in the darkness as if someone is walking down the trail and more than a few are adamant that they saw the apparition of an old man coming after them. According to the story, years ago, an old man lived in some of the many caves at the top of the hill. He hated prostitutes and would go out to some of the city's night spots after dark and kidnap women that he considered to be evil. He would then bring them back up to his home on the hill where he would torture and kill the scarlet women. It is said that after killing these unfortunate women, he would drag their bodies to graves that he had already prepared where he would then bury the evidence of his crimes.

ABANDONED INSANE ASYLUM
Corner of Edith and Osuna
Albuquerque, New Mexico

Figure 14:Interior of the Abandoned Insane Asylum

For whatever reason, it has long been felt that there was something healing about the air in the desert southwest. Perhaps this is the reason that there were so many hospitals and mental asylums built in Albuquerque. As might be suspected, many of these facilities have fallen into disuse.

There is an abandoned house located on the corner of Edith and Osuna that was once an insane asylum. The property is now owned by some of the neighbors who go to great lengths to keep trespassers from entering the property for a variety of reasons. As I made reference to earlier, this empty structure was formerly used as an Insane Asylum and there were several murders committed inside the building by some of the patients.

For those who have risked going into the empty building, it is said that they have sometimes seen a large black cloud hovering in one of the hallways. Interestingly enough, this unusual black cloud has appeared in several photographs taken by some of the more intrepid explorers.

It is also said that one of the patients confined in the building went so crazy that he went on a rampage and killed several other patients and members of the staff. According to the story, after the murders, strange things began to happen in the asylum and many of the staff refused to work after dark. As a result, the management of the Asylum was forced to close it.

At the time the authors researched this location, the neighbors of the deserted building that used to house the insane asylum are members of The Banditos Motorcycle gang. In typical biker fashion, they have made it clear that they would not hesitate to release their Rottweiler on anyone who enters their property or otherwise bothers them.

THE KIMO THEATER
423 Central Avenue
Albuquerque, New Mexico

Figure 15: The KIMO Theater.

The KIMO Theatre, a Pueblo Deco picture palace, opened on September 19, 1927. Pueblo Deco was a flamboyant, short-lived architectural style that fused the spirit of the Native American cultures of the Southwest with the exuberance of Art Deco. Pueblo Deco appeared at a time when movie-mad communities were constructing film palaces based on exotic models such as Moorish mosques and Chinese pavilions.

Native American motifs appeared in only a handful of theatres; of those few, the KIMO is the undisputed king.

Figure 16: The Balcony Stairs Where Bobby Darnall Is Said To Play.

The genius behind the KIMO was Oreste Bachechi, a motivated entrepreneur from humble origins. Oreste Bachechi came to the United States in 1885 and set up a business in a tent near the railroad tracks in Albuquerque. Bachechi's fortunes expanded with the city's growth; he became a liquor dealer and proprietor of a grocery store while his wife Maria ran a dry goods store in the Elms Hotel. By 1919, the Bachechi Amusement Association operated the Pastime Theatre with Joe Barnett. In 1925, Oreste Bachechi decided to achieve "an ambition, a dream that has been long in realization," by building his own theatre, one that would stand out among the Greek temples and Chinese pavilions of contemporary movie mania.

Bachechi envisioned a unique, Southwestern style theatre, and hired Carl Boller of the Boller Brothers to design it. The Bollers had designed a Wild West-Rococo-style theatre in San Antonio and a Spanish cathedral cum Greco-Babylonian interior in St. Joseph, Missouri.

Carl Boller traveled throughout New Mexico, visiting the pueblos of Acoma and Isleta, and the Navajo Nation. After months of research, Carl Boller submitted a watercolor rendering that pleased Oreste Bachechi.

The interior was to include plaster ceiling beams textured to look like logs and painted with dance and hunt scenes, air vents disguised as Navajo rugs, chandeliers shaped like war drums and Native American funeral canoes, wrought iron birds descending the stairs and rows of garlanded buffalo skulls with eerie, glowing amber eyes.

None of the designs were chosen at random. Each of the myriad images of rain clouds, birds and swastikas had historical significance. The swastika is an original Navajo symbol for life, freedom and happiness. Only later was the swastika copied by Hitler for use as a symbol in Nazi Germany. Like its abstract symbols, color, too, was part of the Indian vocabulary. Yellow represents the life-giving sun, white the approaching morning, red the setting sun of the West and black the darkening clouds from the North. The crowning touch was the seven murals painted in oil by Carl Von Hassler. Working from a platform hung from the ceiling, Von Hassler spent months on his creations.

The theatre, which cost $150,000, was completed in less than a year. The elaborate Wurlitzer organ that accompanied the silent films of the day was an extra $18,000. On opening night, an overflow crowd watched performances by representatives from nearby Indian pueblos and reservations. The performers, reported the New Mexico State Tribune in an advance story, included "numerous prominent tribesman of the Southwest who will perform for the audience mystic rites never before seen on the stage."

Isleta Pueblo Governor Pablo Abeita won a prize of $50, a magnificent sum for the time, for naming the new theatre. Reflecting the optimism of the time, "KIMO," is a combination of two words literally meaning "mountain lion" but more liberally interpreted as "king of its kind.

Vivian Vance, who gained fame as Lucille Ball's sidekick in the "I Love Lucy" series, performed at the KIMO. The theatre also hosted such stars as Sally Rand, Gloria Swanson, Tom Mix and Ginger Rogers. When the theatre was packed, the balcony—which spans the east to west walls without support and was designed to give and sway—would drop four to eight inches in the middle.

A year after the realization of his dream, Oreste Bachechi died, leaving the management of the KIMO to his sons, who combined vaudeville and out-of-town road shows with movies. Extra revenue came in from a luncheonette and curio shop on either side of the entrance. In later years, the Kiva-Hi, and second floor restaurant, and KGGM radio, housed on the second and third floors, were major tenants.

In 1951, the boiler in the basement exploded, demolishing a section of the lobby and killing a young boy. Ten years later, a fire destroyed part of the stage area. The movie house then closed in 1968, although the stage is still used by local performing arts groups.

The KIMO fell into disrepair following the exodus from downtown that so many American cities experienced. Slated for destruction, the

KIMO was saved in 1977 when the citizens of Albuquerque voted to purchase this unrivaled palace to movies and one man's dream[7].

THE GHOSTS

There are actually several spirits that seem to haunt this historic old theater. According to those who have had a long association with the KIMO Theater, in 1951 a six-year-old boy named Bobby Darnall was killed when the boiler in the basement exploded, demolishing part of the original lobby. The boiler was located right beneath the concession stand in the lobby.

Figure 17:Headline of death at the KIMO

Bobby, who had been sitting in the theatre balcony with some of his friends, suddenly was frightened by something he saw on the movie screen and ran down the staircase to the lobby. Just as he arrived, the boiler exploded killing little Bobby and completely destroying part of the lobby. It is the spirit of little Bobby who is said to continue to haunt the KIMO Theatre today.

There is also the spirit of an unknown woman, wearing a bonnet that has often been reported walking down the halls of the theatre. She appears to be just going about her business. Nothing more is known of this ghostly presence, but seemingly she doesn't disturb anyone, she just likes strolling about the old theatre.

---

[7] http://www.cabq.gov/kimo/history.html

However, it is the spirit of little Bobby that is a much more prevalent force and has been known to play all kinds of impish tricks upon staff and guests of the old theatre. He is often seen playing on the lobby staircase near the scene of his death. Those who have seen the spirit of little Bobby report that he always wears a striped shirt and blue jeans.

According to the stories told about this old building, the impish spirit of Bobby Darnall causes the performers problems by tripping them and creating a ruckus during performances. To appease the spirit, the cast hangs doughnuts on the water pipe that runs along the back wall of the theatre behind the stage. Often, the treats are gone the next morning. Of those that are left, several people have said that bite marks made by a little mouth, can sometimes be seen.

One year, a crew preparing for a Christmas production took down the stale doughnuts. No sooner were the doughnuts removed, when the technical rehearsal started to become a disaster, with everything going wrong, from lighting, to sound problems, and more. When the treats were replaced, things began to run smoothly again. Staff no longer take chances with rehearsals, as Bobby is well-behaved as long as he has his doughnuts. Now, they stay there.

There are two other entities that seem to be much older than the young boy, seeming to date from the theater's opening night in the fall of 1927. These entities seem to be from that long forgotten era. Very little seems to be known about them.

JOB CORP BUILDING
Albuquerque, New Mexico

Figure 18: Job Corp Facility

The Job Corps Program is a United States Department of Labor no-cost education and vocational training that helps young people ages 16 through 24 get a better job, make more money and take control of their lives.

At Job Corps, students enroll to learn a trade, earn a high school diploma or GED and get help finding a good job. When you join the program, you will be paid a monthly allowance; the longer you stay with the program, the more your allowance will be. Job Corps supports its students for up to 12 months after they graduate from the program.

To be eligible to enroll in Job Corps, students must meet the following requirements:

- Be 16 through 24;

- Be a U.S. citizen or legal resident;

- Meet income requirements;

- Be ready, willing and able to participate fully in an educational environment.

Funded by the United States Congress, Job Corps has been training young adults for meaningful careers since 1964. Job Corps is committed to offering all students a safe, drug-free environment where they can take advantage of the resources provided. Almost all major cities in the United States have a Job Corp presence.

The Jobs Corp Building that houses the Job Corp Offices in Albuquerque, New Mexico is a large warehouse that was a used by a major manufacturing concern in better times. Now it is home to a number of training programs designed to help young people find jobs.

As an addition assist to those preparing for these new jobs, if they have nowhere else to live, the Albuquerque Job Corp has a dormitory on the second floor of the building.

THE GHOSTS

A number of those who have sought to utilize the services offered by the Albuquerque Job Corp have reported that by the lunch room in the building they have seen a nun that is sometimes said to be carrying a baby. It is also said that she can be seen when the lights on the light posts are turned on.

On the girls' side of the new dorms there have been reports of unseen people running up and down the hallway. Even if one of the girls looks out her door as soon as she hears the sounds of running, the hallway is always empty.

MARIA TERESA RESTAURANT & 1840 BAR
618 Rio Grande NW
Albuquerque, New Mexico

Figure 19: The Maria Teresa Restaurant.

The Old Salvador Armijo House, which dates from 1840 is now the Maria Teresa Restaurant and 1840 Bar. The building has a long and varied history as it has been occupied continually since being constructed. A center piece in the Restaurant is the long bar which was originally removed from Fort Sumner, New Mexico and installed in this historic old building in 1970. This 1800s homestead is now the home of a romantic restaurant. The bar has the distinction of having quenched the thirst of, among others, the notorious outlaw Billy the Kid and members of his gang.

THE GHOSTS

This beautiful old hacienda, turned restaurant, is reputed to be one of the most haunted buildings in Albuquerque. According to a news article in the Albuquerque Journal[8], customers often mention the strange energy of the historic building that houses this Old Town restaurant. Owner Rob Spaulding agrees.

"The first time I walked into the Armijo room, I was instantly covered in goosebumps," he says.

Creepy already, the Armijo room is made creepier still by a portrait of Dona Jesusita Salazar de Baca, whose eyes seem to follow you all over the room.

Spaulding says the restaurant is haunted by at least three ghosts — Maria de la Nieves Sarracino, the lady of the house; a youngish woman who wears a red flapper dress; and a mournful male presence, probably the ghost of a man who hanged himself there in the late 1800s. Spaulding says he had one bartender — an ardent nonbeliever — quit immediately after seeing the ghost in the red flapper dress.

The ghost of Maria is the most well-known, according to Daniel Lamb, a 14-year employee of the restaurant and its resident historian. Lamb says Maria's family kept journals, which describe her apparition

---

[8] Wheeler, Liza, <u>N.M. Has Its Share of Haunts</u>, Albuquerque Journal, Thursday, October 31, 2002.

appearing not long after her death. Superstitious, they took down all photos of Maria in the building.

After Maria Teresa's was established, Lamb was invited to examine these family journals. He also got to see a lone photo of Maria — she was wearing a beaded white French dress and had her hair in a bun. Lamb says although there are no portraits of Maria in the building, customers repeatedly describe seeing a woman wearing a beaded white dress walking through the building.

One way Maria apparently amuses herself, Lamb says, is by taking dessert orders — she even brings her own dessert cart. This presents a bit of a problem when an actual member of the wait staff shows up a table and customers say the lady in the beaded gown already took their order.

"I have to explain that the woman was a ghost," Lamb says, "and that the restaurant doesn't own a dessert cart."

As with any house over a hundred years old, there have been a lot of emotions unleashed inside these four walls. These days the Zamora rooms seem to be the most active at the moment. Silverware placed on the tables in this room has been rearranged numerous times to form crosses. The glass shade to a light fixture shattered on its own, however the light bulb inside was not damaged.

In the Armijo Room a glass levitated off the table, flew across the room, hit the wall, bounced back and landed back upon the table. In this same room, another very unusual event was witnessed by the manager and five patrons who were enjoying the fine food served here. According to the reports, a waitress was carrying a tray of water glasses into the room when, one by one, they started exploding.

A number of current and former employees of the Restaurant have reported hearing voices coming from empty rooms and hearing other odd noises as if invisible activity was going on around them. A number of the female employees have also reported experiencing the sensation of being touched by invisible hands.

Others have reported a piano that plays by itself, mirrors that show reflections of ghosts, silverware that moves on its own and many reports of apparitions.

CHILDREN'S PSYCHIATRIC CENTER
University of New Mexico

Figure 20:Children's Psychiatric Center

There are many stories about the Children's Psychiatric Center, but most employees who work there know about the seclusion suite being haunted. Numerous patients who have stayed in the seclusion suite claim they cannot sleep due to visual hallucinations which may actually be ghosts making their presence known.

Most of the employees report have witnessed water turning on and off by itself, lights flickering on and off and doors unlocking or locking without being able to unlock and small black footprints walking across the bathroom floor. In one instance the security cameras were blocked out by a black image and a figure walking towards the camera lens which appeared larger and larger when you looked at the monitor televisions though no explanation for this black image was ever found. Dirty footprints mysteriously appearing on otherwise clean floors, water faucets turning on and off, doors locking and unlocking themselves and shadow figures have been witnessed by the workers at this hospital.

RADISSON HOTEL
Albuquerque, New Mexico

Figure 21: Hotel Cascada/Raddisson Hotel

As might be expected of a city with the age and history of Albuquerque, there are a large number of hotels and motels available to potential travelers. In addition to indoor plumbing, some of the rooms even come with live in spirits. One such hotel is the Radisson Hotel, also known as the Hotel Cascara.

THE GHOSTS

There have been a large number of unusual happenings reported as taking place inside this hotel. Some have reported that while staying on the first floor of the hotel they have heard peculiar scratching noises and the loud slamming of doors from the floor above, even if there was no one renting the room above them.

Others have talked of stories that they have heard about loud yelling and screaming coming from rooms that are vacant and sometimes women who stay in some of these rooms report being shaken from a deep sleep by what seems to feel like children's hands.

All of the floors have been remodeled except the third floor. In fact, guests are not normally permitted on the third floor. A few adventurous souls who have been able to gain access to this floor report that as soon as the elevator doors opened they were hit with a gust of hot air. As they walked further along the hallway on this floor there is an area that was originally outfitted as a bar.

The top of the bar itself is in perfect condition but the rest of it is completely destroyed. Several individual who have had the opportunity to get into this area report that in the corner of the bar was what appears to be newly broken glass. No one had an explanation for the broken glass as the staff rarely goes into the area and none of the windows were broken.

RAMADA HOTEL
10300 Hotel Avenue
Albuquerque, New Mexico

Figure 22: The Ramada Hotel

The Ramada Hotel in Albuquerque is another hotel with a somewhat unusual past and some permanent guests who are not registered at the front desk.

THE GHOSTS

According to some of the hotel staff, one of the spirits resides on the first floor of this large hotel. She said to be a very pretty young broken hearted lady, who was murdered in one of the first floor corner rooms by her lover who wanted her out of his life. She is said to only be on the bottom floor of the hotel, dividing her time between the hotel lobby and the corner room where she was killed.

More than one chamber maid has reported the when housekeeping goes to clean the corner room where the young was murdered that invariably find it in disarray. Among the things reported to have been found in this room are the bed sheets torn off of the bed and thrown onto the floor, the television set knocked onto the floor and the curtains torn from the curtain rods.

This type of activity went on so long in this particular room that finally, the hotel management just closed off the room and do not even make it available for guests. However, out of curiosity, periodically, the staff still visits the room. They always find it is a shambles.

SAN PEDRO PUBLIC LIBRARY
5600 Trumbull Avenue, SW
Albuquerque, New Mexico

Figure 23: San Pedro Library

It has been my experience that many librarians are completely and totally dedicated to their jobs. They love the books and the building in which they are housed. It is also said that many of the librarians centered their lives on the books over which they had charge. So is it any wonder that some of them might return to haunt the library in which they spent most of their lives? There have been a number of reports of lights turning off and on as well as apparitions being seen in various parts of the San Pedro Public Library.

THE GHOSTS

I have had a number of people tell me that late at night, around closing, they have heard strange noises inside this library. Some have even said that they hear footsteps among the shelves and if they forget where they are at and talk to someone near them too loud, they hear a faint shushing as if someone wanted them to lower their voices.

Others have reported hearing the voice of one of the deceased librarians softly asking them to check out a book just as she was wont to do at closing time during her life. I also have in my files reports of several instances where the sounds of giggling were heard in this library as if children are playing among the many shelves of books.

There are also reports of the lights turning off by themselves.

XILINX, INC.
7801 Jefferson Street, NE
Albuquerque, New Mexico

Though they are in a more modern facility today, like many firms have done and will continue to do, the Xilinx Company originally moved into an older building and renovated it to suit their needs. In this particular instance, the old building selected by this computer firm started its life as a mental health hospital. Of course, when this high tech firm purchased this building I am sure they had no intention on also purchasing a ghost.

THE GHOSTS

Former employees and others who have had cause to visit this historic building have reported that on several occasions banging noises have been heard. These sounds seem to echo throughout the building, but they seem to originate in the bathroom. Of course whenever anyone tries to track down the source of the sounds, nothing is ever found.

Others have reported seeing shadowy figures moving up and down the hallways, appearing to duck into rooms whenever someone tries to pursue them. Of course when the would-be ghost chaser dashes into the room the mysterious figures just entered, no one is ever found.

There is an outdoor courtyard from which groaning noises have been heard periodically. Others have heard low pitched voices coming form the back office area. Of course in both cases, investigators never find any sign that anyone caused the groans or the voices. Finally, there have been several instances when objects began to move all by themselves.

LAS MANANITAS
Albuquerque, New Mexico

Figure 24: Las Mananitas

"Las Mañanitas" is a folk song of celebration that is traditionally sung on a person's birthday or Saint's Name Day.

There is no written record of when the adobe structure standing on the northwest corner of present day Indian School and Rio Grande, Albuquerque, NM. was built. Legend and word of mouth has it that parts of the building are over 300 years old.

Paul and Linda took over Las Mañanitas in 1991. Before Paul and Linda, it was a restaurant operated from 1985 to 1990 by a previous Albuquerque Mayor.

Before becoming a restaurant, the property was owned and used as a residence by Sheila Garcia, The Kinneys, The Harrisons and the Gilstraps. There are stories of huge social parties held by previous owners.

Before its use as a residence, verbal history has it remembered as a brothel, saloon and billiards hall. Reportedly the structure was originally built as a stagecoach stop along the historic El Camino Real.

Neighbors and previous owners have told Paul and Linda some of the events and history of the building. At one time there was a farm and a blacksmith located on the property as well. Neighbors would hear the bang and clang of the blacksmith at work.

Original wooden ceiling beams and kiva fireplaces still exist. When the building was renovated in 1991 over five tons of dirt was removed from the original sod roof. There are light fixtures in many rooms and medicine cabinets in both bathrooms that were saved from the famous Albuquerque Hotel Alvarado. (The Alvarado stood from 1896 to 1945.)

Hauntings

Paul and Linda were told when they took over the restaurant in 1991 that it was haunted. In their fourteen years at Las Mañanitas, Paul and Linda have witnessed and been told first hand of several occurrences. There does not seem to be any pattern. The building will be quiet for months at a time then there will be a flurry of unexplained activity for several days in a row.

Reportedly, one previous owner, Mrs. Kinney was plagued by what she thought were 'evil spirits'. She stated that plates flew out of the oven at her and that the doors inside the building would slam shut after she walked through them. The slamming doors unnerved Mrs. Kinney so badly that she had all of the interior doors removed and to this day they remain stacked in the garage.

Supposedly Mrs. Kinney brought in members of the church to perform an exorcism to no avail.

The wait staff employed when Paul and Linda took over the restaurant told them to be sure that they "left toys out for the kids". They were told that the ghosts of a boy and a girl were often seen playing out on the patio or heard playing in the house. Linda leaves toys in hidden areas of the building and then returns to find that they have been somehow broken.

One evening after closing, Paul entered the dining room to find the metal chandelier swinging wildly back and forth. All of the windows and doors were closed in the building, the heat and air conditioning were turned off, and there was no breeze or air flowing in the room. Paul called for Linda to come look. When Linda entered the room she too saw the chandelier swinging from side to side and asked Paul, "What are you doing?!" Paul stated, "I did not do a thing! It was moving when I walked in!" They could not explain the chandelier's movement.

Guests seated in the main dining room have witnessed "something flying in and out of the fireplace". Witnesses state that a "cloud" or "ball of smoke" shot out of the fireplace then moved extremely fast into the center of the room where it dissipated in front of everyone's eyes. One of the guests asked afterwards if they could perform a séance in the room but their request was denied.

Paul and Linda's cat often runs throughout the building as if it is playing with someone. It looks like it is chasing someone or being chased.

Several times Paul and Linda heard what sounded like a squeaky rocking chair rocking bath and forth, in what is now their office, when no one was in the room. A few months later a psychic visited Las Mañanitas.

She asked if she could look around as she felt the presence of "spirits". She walked into what is now their office and told Paul and Linda that she saw a "sewing room with a rocking chair".

The psychic also stated that she felt that a man was hanged in one of the back, older rooms of the building. This is the only mention Paul and Linda have ever heard of a murder or death in the building. The hanging cannot be proved but Paul and Linda state, "given the buildings sordid past, it would not surprise us if it were true!"

The lights go on and off at random. One instance in particular, Paul noticed that the lights in the main dining room were turned off. Paul went and checked the light switch, which is a round dimmer type of switch, and found the switch still turned on. Paul turned the switch off, leaving the lights off, and left the room. A few moments later Paul looked at the dining room and noticed that the lights were now on! He checked the dimmer switch only to find it still in the "off" position. He left the lights on and left the building.

The building is made of adobe and retains heat extremely well. In fact, on hot a summer's day the temperature inside can be quite unpleasant. But at times, the staff will walk through what they describe as unexplainable "really cold spots".

One winter's morning Paul and another employee arrived at work, driving across the virgin snow, almost four inches high, in the parking lot. They were the first to arrive that day. The ground was beautiful with the untouched coating of fresh snow. As they entered the gate to the courtyard they noticed very large footprints in the snow in front of them, walking in a sort of oval route towards the house. However - the tracks seemed to just start and stop with no visible trail leading to or away from them. Paul says the footprints were "Huge - at least a size 14." And that it was "almost as if the person had been placed then lifted off of the ground and disappeared."

One busy afternoon Paul and an employee were frantically cooking in the kitchen. One of the waiters reported to them that they were out of clean coffee cups. The sounds of the dishwasher running and the rattling of dishes could be heard coming from the sink area of the kitchen. Paul assumed that Linda was in back washing dishes and he was a bit upset that she was not out waiting on customers. Just then, Linda walked into the kitchen from the dining room. Paul and the employee both asked, "Well then who is back there doing the dishes?" All three of them heard the noise and rattling coming from the back. They went to look but no one was there. However, they found that all of the coffee cups had mysteriously washed themselves and were drying in the rack.

Customers often ask, out of the blue, if the building is haunted. They state that they 'feel' a presence and that they 'know' it is haunted. Once, a male customer sat out in his car for over an hour and would not join his wife inside for dinner because he felt so uncomfortable.

A professional photographer, Allencort, once visited Las Mañanitas. She took a few pictures around the property. A copy of one of these photos now hangs in the hallway. The copy was sent to Paul and Linda from a Wisconsin Art Gallery where the original photo is on display. Many people report seeing the faint, hidden image of a Grandmother and a Cat in the photo. Allencort returned to Las Mañanitas several times attempting to take more pictures. However, every single photo she shot on subsequent visits never turned out; these photos were completely black.

Paul and Linda believe that there are two main ghosts who haunt Las Mañanitas.

The first is a woman they call 'Priscilla'. Paul and Linda both state that they can "feel her presence". "You know when she is here", they say, "because you can smell her perfume throughout the entire restaurant." The building will be closed with only them in it and the over powering, strong, perfume will fill the air. At other times, customers have even complained about the strong smell.

A Mariachi who often played in the restaurant stated that once he entered the back dining room and saw a woman in a big, fancy, white dress. He looked away for a moment, and when he looked back, she had vanished.

A busboy once saw a blonde haired girl wearing a plaid colored sweater enter the men's bathroom. The bus boy waited and waited for her to exit the bathroom. He knocked on the door and got no answer. He tried the doorknob but it was locked. He waited outside the door for almost an hour then knocked and tried the door again. Now the door was unlocked and when he entered he found the room empty.

The second ghost is that of a large young man. "He is very, very big," states Linda, "But you can tell he isn't that old; he's a young man." He is often seen out of the corner of her eye and Linda often mistakes the shadow for one of the waiters. She will see someone walk by and will call out to who she thinks it is, then she realizes that no one is really there.

Often Linda and other female employees will feel a light breeze blow by them then they feel the touch of fingers on their hips, a friendly and flirty sort of gesture. They will turn around to see who is behind them and no one will be there. Linda even tells the new female wait staff in advance "not to freak out" if this happens to them. One time, a customer felt a hand on her shoulder. When she turned around, no one was there.

The young niece of a frequent customer said that she often talks to 'someone' while in the bathroom of Las Mañanitas. The girl states, "a boy is in there under the floor. He talks to me." When asked how she talked to this boy under the floor she just said, "I don't know - but we communicate." The girl had never heard any of the stories about the shadow of a young man seen in the building.

One afternoon the young girl ran out of the bathroom squealing in excitement, "He told me his name! He told me his name! His name is Joaquin!"

It is believed by many that Priscilla, the woman seen in the fancy white dress, once worked in the brothel that is now Las Mañanitas. Priscilla became pregnant and had her child on the premises. Sadly, Priscilla died while giving birth her son, Joaquin. To this day, Priscilla wanders the halls looking, in vain, for her son just as Joaquin still searches for his Mother.

COVERED WAGON STORE
2034 SOUTH PLAZA
Albuquerque, New Mexico

Figure 25: Covered Wagon Store

This historic building that houses the Covered Wagon Store was once said to have been a private residence and then brothel. The building that was once the home of Manuel Springer is now a store that is believed to be haunted by the apparition of a murdered prostitute named Scarlet.

Mr. Springer was a well-to-do mercantile owner whose business was located next to the house. He was appointed county commissioner in 1904.

After Springer's death, the building, located on the south side of the plaza, was used as a brothel and then as a speakeasy during Prohibition.

In the 1920s, according to legend, Scarlett, a stunningly beautiful lady of the evening, bled to death from a stab wound while waiting for the doctor to complete his poker hand. The ghost of Scarlett has been reportedly seen on the second story of the Springer House balcony, naked except for a garter belt.

ALFREDO'S CAFÉ
Albuquerque, New Mexico

Figure 26: Alfredo's Coffee Shop

There are a number of rumors about Alfredo's Café. There have been many reports of strange occurrences in this quaint Mexican Restaurant from electrical problems to guests reporting that they are positive that they are being watched by unseen entities. According to legend, this building is haunted by a Spanish soldier.

PRIVATE RESIDENCE
Four Hills Area
Albuquerque, New Mexico

The residence is located in the Four Hills area of Albuquerque and is a two story single family dwelling with attached garage. The reporting party asks that we use only her first name in any web posts and do not specifically state her address.

Ashley has lived in the house for 2 1/2 years and states that there have been noises from upstairs since the beginning of occupancy. Since one year ago there has been an increase in activity. The house is 33 years old and has had three owners. Very little is known about the history of the house, except that a "mostly cosmetic" (floors, ceilings, paint) remodel was done about three years ago. The remodel did include some electrical work in the form of ceiling fan installations. The house is for sale and has been on the market for about a month. No electricians or plumbers have been called to determine possible causes of the reported phenomena.

- General noises in upstairs section of house, mostly resembling footsteps or running children. The most common noise is the sound of running towards the master bedroom followed by rattling of the master bedroom doorknob.
- Locked doors will unlock and open themselves.
- Faucets will turn on by themselves.
- The bed in the master bedroom will shake, often enough to wake the occupant. This happens usually at night.
- Lights will turn themselves on.
- DVD player cords will unplug themselves.

- Orbs appear in pictures taken inside the house.

- A bizarre phone message was once left on the resident's voice mail. The speaker's voice was unintelligible, but seemed to transition from a little girl's voice to an angry man's voice. A tape of the message is not available, but was heard by witnesses present at the investigation.

- Reported phenomena are "worse" when a group is in the house, and generally take place in the upstairs section of the house. Other witnesses present at the time of the investigation have observed most forms of the reported phenomena.

Previous Investigations/Interventions

Two "cleansings" were performed on April 4 and November 8 of 2003 by P. Burns, apparently a local person representing herself as a psychic or spiritual healer. Ms. Burns charged a substantial sum of money for each "cleansing" but the reported phenomena continued.

Heather, a friend of the resident, once burned sage and asked the "spirits" to leave. This reportedly made things worse. A Ouija board was also used to attempt contact with those responsible for the phenomena. No messages were received, but one person interviewed stated the board made a partial message along the lines of "you're not welcome."

Personal Interview of Reporting Party

The reporting party is a health care professional having a doctoral degree. She denies any current health problems. Her medical history is notable for head trauma (concussion) sustained in the course of a motor vehicle accident in 1991 but which has been asymptomatic since initial recovery. She reports no visual or audio hallucination since the injury; she also reports no history of habitual illicit drug use. Answers to questions about mental health were given readily and were unremarkable. Her family history is notable for the death of a close family member nine years ago; the reporting party does not make any connection between this death and the reported phenomena. She states she has tried making both friendly and firm statements to the ghosts to leave her alone, but this has not helped.

Witness Statements

Several friends of the reporting party were present at the time of the investigation. All reported witnessing several instances of the above reported phenomena both alone and in the company of others. Some reported smelling blood in the house; a ringing in the ears was also reported.

Significant Instrument Readings

A 5 mGa increasing to 7 mGa reading at the top of the stairs. A photo taken at the time of the reading reveals an orb.

An off scale reading was reported on the master bedroom floor very close to the bed, running in a line across the room. This was eventually traced to an electrical line apparently installed along with two ceiling fans on the first floor.

EVP recordings were made in both the master bedroom and a now vacant guest bedroom.

A definite, strong EM field is located in the master bedroom, and traced to a recently installed electrical line. The master bedroom is the source of much of the reported phenomena, however since the house is currently for sale no corrective action was recommended.

LUNA-OTERO MANSION
The restaurant is twenty miles south of Albuquerque off I-25 in Las Lunas. Albuquerque/Las Lunas, New Mexico

Figure 27: The Luna-Otero Mansion.

Even though the Luna-Otero Mansion is not inside the city limits of Albuquerque, it is close enough to that city and so involved in the history of the area that the distinction of being located in Las Lunas is really not important.

In 1692 Domingo de Luna came to New Mexico on a land grant from the King of Spain.   A few years later, Don Pedro Otero came to Valencia County under similar circumstances. These two families grew, acquired fortunes in land and livestock, and became extremely powerful in politics and prominent in territorial society. The family heads became friends and business associates. The marriages of Solomon Luna to Adelaida Otero, and Manuel A. Otero to Eloisa Luna in the late 1800's united these two families into what became known as the Luna-Otero Dynasty.

In 1880 the Santa Fe Railroad wanted right-of-way through the Luna property. In return for this favor, and because the proposed railroad tracks went squarely through the existing Luna hacienda, the railroad agreed to build a new home to the specifications of Don Antonio Jose and his family. Legend has it that numerous trips through the South by the Luna family inspired the architectural design of the mansion. Whether or not this is true, the building is unique in that, while it is southern colonial in style, its basic construction material is adobe.

Figure 28: Another view of the Luna Otero Mansion

Because Don Antonio Jose died in 1881, the first family to occupy the mansion was his oldest son, Tranquilino. After Don Tranquilino's death in Washington while serving in the legislature, younger brother Solomon took the reins of the family. Although Solomon was probably the most famous of the Lunas, he was not very prolific. With no children in his family, control passed to his nephew, Eduardo Otero, in the early 1900's. It was during this time, specifically in the 1920's that the mansion truly became the outstanding building that now exists. During this period the solarium was constructed, the front portico was added, and the ironwork, which once surrounded about five times as much property as it now does, was erected. Responsible for these and other improvements was a talented and creative woman, Josefita Manderfield Otero, wife of Don Eduardo. Josefita, or Pepe as she is affectionately remembered, was a daughter of

William R. Manderfield, founder of the Santa Fe New Mexican. This fine lady ruled the mansion with a gentle and loving hand and spent her days caring for her magnificent gardens and applying paint to canvas. There are those in this area who still remember and speak highly of her.

The words "Los Lunas" in Spanish means, where the Lunas live. Before the arrival of the Santa Fe Railroad, Los Lunas identified a geographic location of the family's ranch headquarters and home. Growth as a town, and bustling bedroom community to Albuquerque that it is today, began after the railroad arrived.

THE GHOSTS

I can find no record of hauntings in this historic old home until the 1970's when the grand old mansion was remodeled into a restaurant. It was then that the ghost of one of the original family members, Josefita "Pepe" Otero, began to appear. Several employees have seen her ghost and describe her as very real looking, dressed in 1920's clothing. She haunts two former bedrooms on the second floor an attic storeroom and the top of the stairs which leads to the second floor bar.

One of the stories of the hauntings in this old home concerns the old rocking chair, which sits at the top of the stairs. Several employees have reported seeing the spectral figure of a woman seated in this chair, rocking slowly, as if she was taking a leisurely break. She looked so real that one evening one employee approached the figure as she sat peacefully rocking. Seeing the young man approaching, the woman stood up, then slowly vanished. This particular spirit has been seen many places in the restaurant, and many believe that it is Josefita, who still visits her old home.

It was also reported to me that one of the waitresses in the upstairs serving area had some encounters. According to the young woman in question, one evening she saw a man sitting quietly on one of the sofas, as if he was waiting to be served. She said that the man was dressed oddly. His clothing was more in keeping with what was worn many years ago. She also thought it somewhat unusual that he was not complaining about the fact that the staff seemed to be ignoring him. The waitress asked one of the other staff members why the man hadn't been served, and the other person said, "What man?" When the waitress looked over to the couch, the man just faded away.

The stairway that leads from the front door up to the second floor is a favorite place for Josefita. She walks up and down the stairs, and has been seen by employees and patrons alike. It was reported that one evening, the spirit of this indomitable old lady walked across the main downstairs dining room as if she owned the place. Of course, if it is the spirit of Josefita, she once did own the place. Why should death change that?

I must warn those who think to go to this historic old house to ghost hunt that I received a very cold reception when I went. When I identified myself to the owners I was informed very rudely that they were Christians and did not believe in ghosts and I was not even welcome to have a meal there. So much for Christian charity. It has been my experience of all the religions I have come in contact with that so-called Christians are often times the least Christian of all.

THE WOOL WAREHOUSE THEATER RESTAURANT
502 1st Street, NW
Albuquerque, New Mexico

Figure 29: Wool Warehouse

The Wool Warehouse Theater Restaurant began its life as a wool warehouse. Like most buildings in older area of America's larger cities that are being considered for renovation and preservation of the historic buildings, this old building is now being used for something totally different than the purpose for which it was built.

In 1984, this abandoned old warehouse was purchased and converted into a dinner theater. Now the floors that used to groan under the weight of heavy bales of cotton resound to the sounds of the footsteps of the many customers that enjoy coming to this eatery and the wait staff that hurry from table to table. The stage area also now is a busy place as the actors and stage hands work to produce entertaining plays.

THE GHOSTS

In this particular instance, no one seems to know the identity of the spirit that haunts this historic building. However, no one seems to doubt his existence as he has been seen many times.

The unidentified ghost that seems fascinated by the plays that are part of the dinner theater entertainment is that of a man wearing a double breasted, cream colored suit. He has been observed by both customers as well as the actors standing near the stage during performances. Cold spots have also been reported in this same area, as well as the feeling of an unseen presence in the area around the stage.

CHURCH STREET CAFÉ
2111 Church Street
Albuquerque, New Mexico

Figure 30: Church Street Cafe

Another haunted location in Albuquerque is the Church Street Café, built in 1709 as the home of the Ruiz family. This renovated 18 room hacienda is nestled in the shadows of the San Felipe de Neri Catholic Church and is the site of continuing unexplained activities.

There are those who say that Sara Ruiz is the cause of the hauntings in this historic old building. Sara was said to be a healer, well versed in the use of the many herbs that she collected. The locals could probably have tolerated this activity, as many placed more faith in homespun medicine than they did the early doctors of the area.

However, it was Sara's views on the conventions of the day that seems to have caused much of the gossip about her. She was definitely an unconventional woman. In a day and age when. A proper woman married before having children, Sara never did marry, though she seems to have produced a large brood of children. In fact, one of her children was the last of the Ruiz family to live in this beautiful old home. After the death of Rafinia Ruiz, the home was sold by the Ruiz family to Marie Coleman, the current owner of the Church Street Café.

Of course, what no one thought to tell Marie was that Sara Ruiz had never left her former dwelling. A number of vents that have occurred convinced Marie that Sara Ruiz never got around to leaving the house she grew up in — despite being dead for more than a century.

It was during the renovation Marie had her first brush with Sara. Since the old house required a great deal of renovation before it could be opened at the Church Street Café, Marie interviewed a number of contractors. TO her surprise, while she was taking one through the house, she could hear a woman's angry voice shouting at her to get that man out of the house at once.

Marie said later that she could feel the anger all around her as they moved from room to room and she rushed the contractor through the house barely giving him a chance to look at the work that needed to be done. Once outside the house, everything became calm. Marie had no idea who had been shouting at her, but she knew this man could not work on the house. She later learned that the prospective contractor was the grandson of a man Sara had been involved with long ago.

Marie finally convinced a friend to handle the work for her. She never mentioned the woman's voice she'd heard until the new contractor finally told her she'd have to do something about "that woman." "Tell her to stop kicking the buckets around," he told her. "Make her stop." Marie couldn't believe it, but Charlie was well aware of Sara. She asked just how she was supposed to stop her. He replied, "Talk to her."

Marie took his advice, and the spirit stopped kicking the buckets. That was the beginning of their relationship. Marie believes the spirit is Sara Ruiz and Marie gives her the room and respect the donia deserves. She greets her every morning and bids her good bye every night. Now and then, when Sara wants her attention, she tosses small pebbles at Marie. A waiter told Marie he saw the spirit of Sara in a long black dress, and customers have said they've felt a presence.

When Marie's brother Jim came in to help her, he would have none of this ghost nonsense. On the first night he locked up alone, he couldn't find his keys. The door was already locked, but he needed the keys to get out. He knew where he'd put them, but they weren't there. As he began an all-out search, he heard a voice laughing. "All right, Sara," he said. "Leave me alone." He found the keys in his pocket. When he got to the door, it was unlocked. He quickly became a believer.

A number of people have said that they have seen Sara Ruiz performing daily chores — like feeding ghost chickens out back — and, at closing time, she is fond of engaging the owner in a battle of light switches: Marie Coleman turns them off, and Ruiz turns them on, ad nauseum.

There is a locked glass case in the lobby that contains figurines and pottery. There is one figurine from a nativity scene that Sara Ruiz apparently hates. Most mornings, when Marie Coleman arrives at work, that figurine is in a different position from where it was the night before. Sometimes, Coleman says, the figurine has been moved to the very edge of the glass shelf, so she has to maneuver carefully to keep it from falling when she opens the door. The employees all swear that they have not moved the figurines.

HIGH NOON RESTAURANT AND SALOON
425 San Felipe MW
Albuquerque, New Mexico

Figure 31: High Noon Restaurant and Saloon

Another haunted building in Albuquerque's Old Town is a building that was originally built in 1785. During its long life, this historic old building has served as both a casino as well as a very successful brothel. Now it is the High Noon Restaurant and Saloon.

There are those who believe that this popular restaurant/saloon is haunted by the spirit of a trapper, who may responsible for customers and employees feeling a tap on the shoulder by an unseen presence or smelling the fireplace burning when it's not.

The ghost is often absent for long stretches, but when he is in residence, the spirit makes himself known by rattling dishes and, disconcertingly, calling out the wait staff's names.

The building in which the foyer and Santo room of the High Noon Saloon are located is one of the original structures in historic Old Town Albuquerque.

August 20, 1850, is listed in the building's original territorial deed as the date of the first recorded sale of the building, when Quereva Griego De Chavez purchased it from Jose Delores Chavez. It changed owners four additional times between 1884 and 1965 when the present owner, George Sandoval, purchased the building from Carlos Vigil. Leonardo Huning, whose family built the famous Huning Castle which stood nearby on Central Avenue for many years, owned the structure from 1887 to 1894.

LA PINATA
2 Patio Market Street NW
Albuquerque, New Mexico

According to what I can find out, the building that houses the La Pinata once housed a school. The ghost that haunts this location is believed to be that of a very hungry little boy who attended this school. There were apparently a number of spirits who once visited this location, but after one became especially violent, a cleansing ceremony was held in order to eject the spirits. Now only the little boy seems to be in residence.

There seem to be several areas of disturbance within the structure. In the bathroom there have been a number of electrical problems. This might be expected in an old building, but it seems to be very intermittent. In a back storeroom, an unseen presence knocked the owner off of a ladder. This event might mean that the violent spirit has not left, but is now much weaker in ability.

I am also told that the owner left a bowl of candy on the counter one evening as an offering to the little boy. When the owner left, the bowl was full of candy. The next morning, the owner, who was the first on to arrive, noticed that the bowl was half empty. Apparently the little boy enjoyed the candy.

LA PLACITA RESTAURANT
208 San Felipe Street NW
Albuquerque, New Mexico

Figure 32: La Placita.

The building that houses the La Placita Restaurant was supposedly built around 1706 by Don Juan Armijo y Maestas and then later sold to Ambrosio Armijo. The building was constructed as what is called the classic placita (little plaza) style, developed for defense against raiding by Indian War Parties as well as various military units that fought across the desert southwest over its turbulent history.

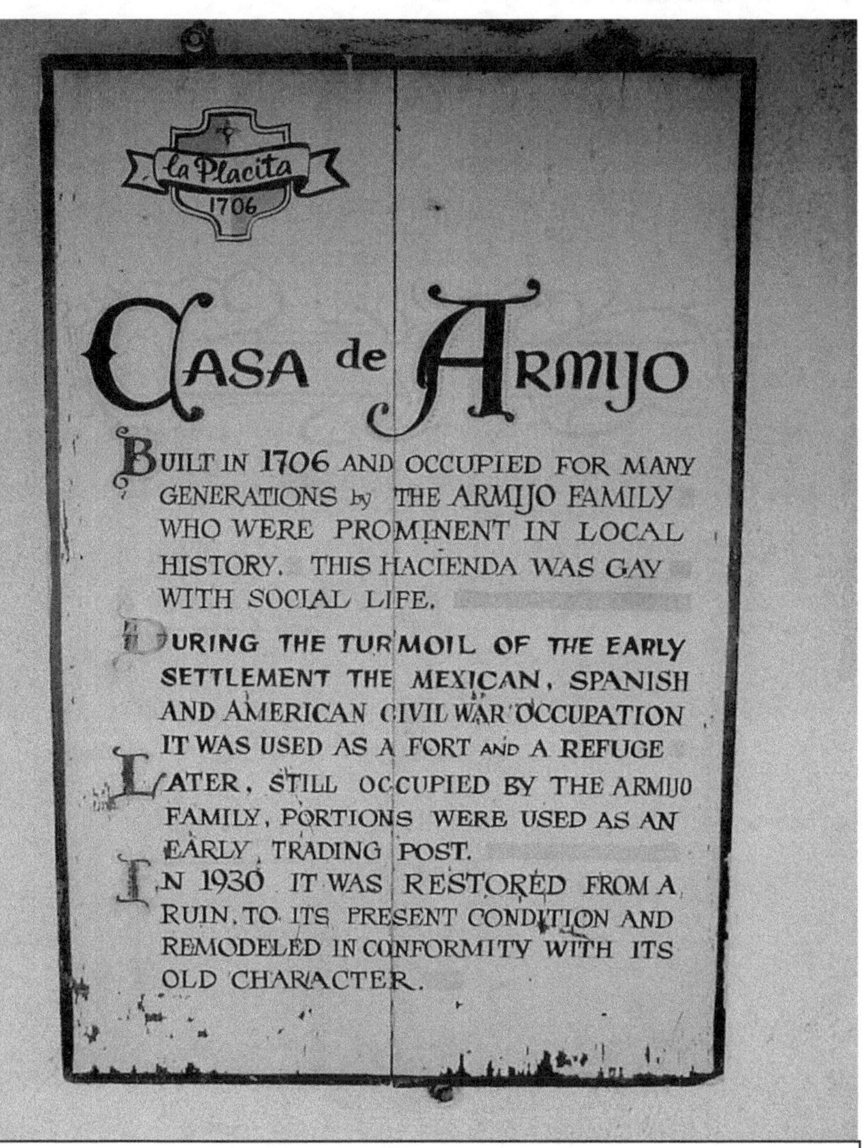

Figure 33: The History of La Placita.

According to the many stories about this historic old building, it is believed that the Casa Armijo is haunted by at least four different spirits, according to those who have worked at the restaurant. All would agree that the vast majority of reported phenomena seem to occur in the women's restroom and the upstairs area.

Almost everyone who would talk about their adventures at the former Casa de Armijo agree that it is was almost routine that they would hear their names called by someone who sounded as if they stood very close to them. When they would turn around the answer the call, there would be no one there.

A number of female employees would see the apparition of a young girl reflected in the mirrors of the women's restroom. When they would turn around to see who the young girl was, there would be no one in the restroom but themselves. Several who had experienced then reported that what is now the women's restroom was once a part of the bedroom of one of the young Armijo girls who is said to have died in the room of an unknown disease in the early 1900's.

Several people reported that they experienced cold spots can be felt at certain times throughout various locations in the building. Glowing lights have been seen floating in the hallways on the second floor near the manager's office.

JOHNSON GYM
UNIVERSITY OF NEW MEXICO

Figure 34: Johnson Gym

This haunted site is interesting in that almost every university I have written about has a ghost of some sort associated with the University Pool. However, be that as it may, there are a number of stories about Johnson Gym being haunted by a girl who either committed suicide or was murdered.

There's an urban legend telling the story of a student who took her own life in the locker room over a failed romance. Some have said to have heard her weeping. One has even said that she was touched on her shoulder by such ghost.

Others say that a murder took place in Johnson Gym. The story seems to be that a young woman was raped and murdered. Unfortunately, like so many other stories of this type, there is little evidence to confirm the events. Still - - - - - .

BOTTGER KOCH MANSION
110 San Felipe Street NW
Albuquerque, New Mexico

Figure 35:Entrance to the Bottger-Koch Mansion

The Bottger Mansion has a storied history, involving famous entertainers (Elvis, Sinatra), one known mobster (Machine Gun Kelly), and three ghosts who still visit frequently. The Mansion has won numerous awards and has been featured on PBS and QVC television programs. This year, an award-winning gladiator with a beautiful mind has spent time at the Mansion.

Construction was started in 1905 and completed within two years. Charles Bottger was a wool exporter originally from Germany who made his fortune after migrating to New Jersey. He moved to New Mexico – close to the Native American sheep ranchers– and built the Bottger Mansion in Old Town. There were four original mansions in Old Town, and only the Bottger remains, intact, virtually as it was when built.

Charles Bottger owned a saloon west of the Mansion (now the parking lot) and a toll bridge over the Rio Grande River. His saloon advertised "Fine Whiskeys, Fine Cigars, Fine Women and Billiards."

The Mansion was used as living quarters by three generations of Bottgers, then sold several times.

During the forties it was used as a home for a small colony of Buddhists. Later it was used as a restaurant downstairs, a boarding house and beauty salon upstairs. In 1955, a young Elvis Presley (along with Bill Black and Scotty Moore) performed two shows in Albuquerque and stayed at the Bottger, leaving the next day for a show in Amarillo.

In the late 50's, a prominent Italian family rented the Bottger for a large wedding. Frank Sinatra was a guest, who performed in the courtyard after the wedding dinner was served.

In the 40's, the FBI's Most Wanted criminal, Machine Gun Kelly, was being hunted by lawmen everywhere. Kelly, his girlfriend and his gang were headed back to Memphis from California and checked into the Bottger under assumed names. They had dyed their hair and purchased new clothes to help conceal their identities. After several days, the owners became suspicious when they noticed that the group always sent a neighborhood boy out to purchase the meals and bring them back to the Bottger for consumption in the rooms. They decided to notify the police, but were overheard by one of the gang members. They quickly left just ahead of the law. However, they were captured shortly thereafter and imprisoned.

The Garcia family purchased the Bottger and converted it to a B&B in the 80's. They did a great business for many years, before selling it to the Koch family in 1997. The Koch's changed the name to the Bottger-Koch Mansion during their ownership. The previous owners, Gary and Carole Millhollon purchased it from the Koch's in 2003, and reverted to the original, historic name. Steve and Kathy Hiatt purchased the Mansion in 2004.

THE GHOSTS

Depending on which past owner (or Old Town resident) you speak to, there are at least three ghosts (and some say six) living in the Bottger.

All are harmless, but do play pranks. "The Old Man" (whom many assume is Charles himself) is a regular. He will occasionally pace in the parlor or stairway, usually late at night.

The "Grandmother" ghost just sighs. She is most often heard in the Linda Lee and the Carole Rose suites. No one has ever reported seeing her, but many, many guests report hearing her sigh from time to time. Some believe that she is Charles' granddaughter who died as a very old lady and lamented the fact that her children intended to sell the property after her death (which they did).

One story has it that they locked her out of the house one night after her bath; she caught pneumonia, and died, thus assuring their inheritance.

The "Lover Ghost" is often featured in the Old Town Ghost Tour. He reportedly joins young, pretty women in the bedrooms at night. Since we've been owners, no guests have reported his presence, but stories are legend about his past visits in which he just wants to lie down next to the young ladies. When they turn on the light to see who has joined them, no one is there.

The famous Ghost Detectives of Los Angeles rented the Bottger for a week and explored the many ghosts in Old Town including the ones here in the Mansion. Their visit, complete with strange electrical devices, recorders of all types, and special photographic equipment can be reviewed over the internet. According to them, there are "at least 4, and perhaps more, ghosts living in the Bottger Mansion.

This bed and breakfast has it all: flying objects, strange sounds, cold spots, mysterious smells (like men's cologne or rose toilet water) and apparitions.

Owner Yvonne Koch says one morning a guest came down with pieces of a soap dish in her hands. The rattled guest swore that she didn't break it — she saw it go flying across the bathroom and crash into the wall.

Koch confesses she feels the ghosts more often than seeing them. She says there are six spirits at the mansion, including a native woman who fell down the stairs to her death; Charles and Miquela Bottger; and their daughter Dorothy Bottger, who died from pneumonia after being locked out of the house.

There have also been a number of other manifestations that have been reported. Such as:

- A dessert plate on a top shelf levitated up and fell to the floor

- Cold spots have been felt while sitting in the chair in the lobby.

- The toilet lid in the downstairs bathroom moves and objects on top of it fly off and across the room.

- One guest reported a "white fog" that came under the door to her room and tried to enter her mouth.

- Guests have reported the feeling of an unseen person breathing on their arms.

- The apparition of a woman has been seen on the first floor.

BERNALILLO COUNTY COURTHOUSE
Albuquerque, New Mexico

Bernalillo County was established 8 January 1852. It was one of the seven Partidos, established during Mexican rule. It may have been named for the Gonzales-Bernal family that lived in the area before 1692. The county seat is Albuquerque.

The first courthouse in Albuquerque was built in 1886 at a cost of $62, 053.81 and was constructed of gray stone with a peaked shingled roof exterior tower reaching three stories high. The courthouse stood at the current San Felipe Elementary School site in Old Town. Once the demand for another school surfaced, the Bernalillo County Courthouse was relocated to New Town (present day downtown area).

This "new" courthouse was built in 1926 with bricks imported from Colorado. Built in the center of its own park, the symmetrical design gave the building a Grecian, temple of justice effect. In 1964, the courthouse was remodeled and expanded. Its outer surface was also refinished with sheets of marble. A more modern courthouse was built and completed in 2001, leaving the older building empty. At least empty of human workers, but there are still the stories of figures moving through empty halls going on about their duties.

THE GHOSTS

In 2003 the Community Service Group has been cleaning out the old courthouse downtown. In the basement rooms they've been collectively witnessing strange things. A worker reported seeing a little girl standing in one of the dark halls; she was a blonde with braids, wearing a school uniform. When the witness smiled at the little girl, she vanished.

A cold spot in another hall was experienced by the lead-man himself. He was unable to find a vent or source to explain it. All of the JDC "clients" that were doing the CS work were taking a break in one of the rooms, and an old law book circa 1920's went skittering down the hall. It came to a stop in the cold zone. Nobody's been willing to touch it.

Two people reportedly died in the building - both of heart attacks. A Sheriff at his desk in the basement and another man on an upper floor both died in this manner. Reportedly employees have tried doing little 'tests' - placing objects in certain places and placing a dry eraser on a door knob, etc and then returning to find these objects moved.

Other things that have been experienced by visitors are cold spots, hot spots, lights being turned off, doors being closed and locked when a key is required and boxes that were taped closed being opened and contents strewn about.

QUARAI MISSION
Mountainair, New Mexico

The ruins of Quarai are southeast of Albuquerque in the Manzanos Mountains at Punta de Agua. Whenever I think ab out Albuquerque, I see these ruins in my mind's eye. As a result, I decided to include them in this volume.

As with the Luna-Otero Mansion, the ruins of the Quarai Mission are very close to the city of Albuquerque. This is another reason that I am including them in the Albuquerque section of this book.

Quarai was a thriving pueblo when Don Juan Oñate first approached it in 1598 to "accept" its oath of allegiance to Spain. Since Onate was on a journey of exploration and treasure hunting, giving its "oath" to the King of Spain would probably have made little difference to the inhabitants of this area except along with Onate came the dreaded Inquisition. Unfortunately for the natives, the Spanish decided that Quarai was a good spot for a Mission.

Three of the Spanish priests assigned to the Quarai Mission were head of the New Mexico Inquisition during the 1600s, including Fray Estevan de Perea, Custodian of the Franciscan order in the Salinas Jurisdiction and called by one historian the "Father of the New Mexican Church." Despite the horrors associated with the word "Inquisition," records from the hearings show that the early inquisitors, in New Mexico at least, were compassionate men capable of separating gossip from what the church regarded as serious transgressions.

Figure 36: Quarai Mission

In one case, tensions between church and state reached a peak when Perea charged the alcalde (mayor) of Salinas with encouraging the native Kachina dances. That case was dropped, but the alcalde's continued disruption at the mission prompted the Inquisition to banish him. Quarai was the base of operations for the Inquisition here in New Mexico.

What appear to be low hills around the ruins are actually the remains of a large masonry Indian village or pueblo. The few scattered walls above ground are the results of limited excavations in the 1950s. There has been little archeological research in the pueblo, so we only the barest outline of Quarai's prehistory is currently known. From ground surveys of the area, and occasional mention in Spanish records, it would appear that the population of Quarai in the 1600s was around four hundred to six hundred people. Not all of the house blocks were occupied at the same time; some were abandoned while others were thriving.

Quarai was on the southeastern fringe of the pueblo world. Tiwa-speaking Indians migrated through mountain canyons from the area around present-day Albuquerque before A.D. 1300. They established settlements along the eastern slope of the Manzano Mountains at Chilili, Tanique, and here at Quarai.

The inhabitants of this area farmed, hunted, and gathered salt from saline lakes in the valley beyond. They also took advantage of their location between Rio Grande pueblos and the Plains Indians to become traders.

Figure 37: Inside the Mission.

Also called the church of Nuestra Senora de La Purisima Concepcion de Cuarac, enduring symbol of the early Spanish presence in this valley. Quarai is probably a later phonetic spelling of Cuarac. The red sandstone walls, once protected by adobe plaster, are forty feet high on foundations seven feet deep and six feet wide. The interior length of the church is one hundred feet. The nave is twenty-seven feet wide, and the transept fifty feet.

Since we have no plans or drawings of these early Franciscan missions, we must envision how they looked by studying the physical clues which remain. The square holes above the entry are sockets for beams. They hint that a porch extended across the front of the church, although no traces of it remain. The splayed entrance held wide doors which swung inward on iron pivot hinges providing light and easy access.

It is believed that Fray Juan Gutierrez de la Chica, a priest assigned her in 1628 probably started construction of the church. Although Quarai was on a frontier, remote from the hearth of the Spanish Empire and the Catholic Church, every detail of the church's conception and construction reveal careful planning and attention.

These massive stone walls enclosed a vast space which contrasted sharply with the modest rooms familiar to the Indians. The kiva located nearby is a ceremonial chamber of the pueblo religion. This kiva is a shape more familiar than the square kiva in the patio of the convento. However, in Tiwa pueblos both square as well as round kivas are common. The flat roof of a kiva was supported by posts. On the floor was a fire pit, and the hatchway above served as both an entrance and an opening for smoke to escape. As warm air and smoke rose out the hatchway, cool air descended through a ventilator shaft on the east side. Thus fresh air circulated through the kiva making it a reasonably comfortable place for the various activities carried out below.

This kiva was here before the church and convento were built. It was buried by mission construction, implying that the Spanish structures were built on a mound of pueblo ruins similar to those you see along the trail today. It was never in use during the mission period.

The architectural contrast between these Tiwa and Spanish structures is clear; and it suggests an even greater gulf between the social and spiritual worlds of the cultures which created them. Oddly enough, this is where we obtained the majority of our unusual readings. By the 1670s, the people of Quarai were suffering all the problems of drought, disease, famine, and hostile tribes that plagued the Salinas Jurisdiction as a whole.

As a result of the drought and the illness, coupled with the inability of the Procurator General to send sufficient supplies, in 1677 Fray Parraga made the decision to abandon the mission and move his charges to another area.

Today these ruins yield clues to the relationships between Spaniards and the Salinas pueblos. What affect the Spanish had upon pueblo life is also hinted at by the archeological information unlocked here at Quarai. Many remnants of life in that time still survive as part of the cultural tradition that is New Mexico today.

THE GHOSTS

Along with a vast feeling of age, it is said that this seventeenth century mission is haunted by the ghost of a conquistador that still guards the ruins. There are many who claim to at least know someone that has seen this relic of a bygone age. It is said that he enters through one of the gaps in the adobe walls and is surrounded by a blue white light. He wears a tabard bearing the symbol of the Calatrava, a Spanish military religious group.

This ghost of the conquistador was first reported in 1913. The first to see him was startled when the man from the past pointed his finger at a startled tourist and said (in Spanish): "Frequent this place, traveler on a mystic journey."

Since that time, not only the conquistador but several dark clothed monks have been seen moving about the ruins.

Rancho de Corrales
Corrales, New Mexico

Figure 38: Entrance to Rancho Corrales

This Rancho Corrales is not actually in Albuquerque, but about 15 miles north of the city, in Corrales, New Mexico. This gracious old hacienda was built in 1801 by Diego Montoya. The sprawling adobe home, with its thick walls and heavily timbered ceilings was, at first, a peaceful oasis surrounded by orchards. However, that all changed when the Luis and Louisa Emberto purchased the property in 1883. Some five years after they moved in, a bloody shootout occurred. It all started when Luis discovered that his wife was having an affair and moved out of the hacienda promising to return and kill both her and her lover. On April, 1898, made good on his promise and shot his wife twice.

An armed posse soon surrounded the hacienda and in the gun battle that ensued, Luis was struck down. Due to the scandalous circumstances of the couple's death, they were not allowed a proper burial in the church cemetery and as a result their remains were interred across the irrigation ditch to the west of the building.

Today, the restless pair continues to make their presence known at the hacienda turned restaurant. Reported activities include items that seemingly move on their own, the sounds of disembodied voices, and the appearance of a woman in 1800's era clothing. Others have heard the sound of midnight parties in the old hacienda.

HOTEL PARC CENTRAL
Albuquerque, New Mexico

Figure 39:Hotel Parq Central

The Hotel Parq Central is boutique hotel that offers both historic elegance and contemporary comfort. Guestrooms (of which there are 74, including 15 luxury suites and 3 spacious cottages) are each stylishly appointed. In your room you'll enjoy high ceilings, large windows, rich fabrics, and custom designed furniture that compliments the inviting ambience.

Opening in 1926, the building was named Santa Fe Hospital, and was used for the treatment of the employees of the Atchison, Topeka & Santa Fe Railway Company. In the 40's the hospital was renamed AT & SF Hospital, and later, in the 80's, it was purchased by a group of psychiatrists and renamed Memorial Hospital. For the next three decades it was a place where children and young adults suffering from mental conditions were treated. It wasn't until 2010, after a huge $21 million investment, and support from the city and the Huning Highland Historic District Neighborhood Association, that the Hotel Parq Central opened its doors. This one-time psychiatric hospital and continued cultural icon in the area, has decades of history, with many reports of the paranormal throughout the years.

Several of these incidents occurred during the time the building was known as Memorial Hospital. Many patients have had their own experiences including the sighting of apparitions. The top floor on the right wing is where a woman apparition has been watching people in the hallways. Patients also reported having their bedsheets pulled off them in the middle of the night.

Patients have stated that they've been so traumatized by some of the events in this ex-hospital, that once discharged they have continued to suffer from nightmares about the building.

Patients were not the only ones to experience things that couldn't be explained, staff of the hospital did too. They would often have the sensation of being watched, as well as hearing something whisper in their ear, the movement of objects, and a general sense of heaviness throughout the buildings.

During an investigation in January 2011 by the Los Muertos Spirit Seekers, three team members are said to have experienced unexplained voices/whispering close to their location. They also reported distinct coldness near their body, and a sense of being watched. After reviewing their evidence, some of these experiences were captured on digital voice recorders. They also carried out the flashlight technique – an attempt at communication with a spirit that involves the answering of questions through the turning on of the flashlight. This was a success, with several responses captured on video.

Casa de Fiesta Restaurant, Albuquerque, NM

Figure 40: Casa De Fiesta Restaurant

The Casa de Fiesta Restaurant is another of the quaint restaurants to be found in Albuquerque's Old Town. But the employees of the restaurant believe that they may have a ghost. The typical otherworldly encounters that are discussed include disembodied voices and unexplainable noises coming from the trap door in the main dining room. There have also been stories of employees and customers seeing figures out of the corner of their eyes that vanish then they look for them.

FAIRFIELD MEMORIAL PARK
700 Yale Blvd SE
Albuquerque, New Mexico

Figure 41: Fairfield Memorial Park

The Fairfield Memorial Park Cemetery is at the corner of Yale and Avenida Chavez in Albuquerque and it is the oldest public cemetery in the City. Various rumors surround the older section of the cemetery that range from sightings of apparitions to the practice of necromancy. The most interesting reports have come from passing motorists who claim to have witness apparitions in the cemetery that suddenly vanish.

Capilla de Nuestra Senora de Guadalupe Chapel, Albuquerque, NM

Figure 42: Capilla de Neustra Senora de Guadalupe Chapel

Patio Escondido Mall in Old Town, Albuquerque was once home to the Sagrada, a sacred arts school founded by Dominican Sister Giotto Moots in 1969. Sister Giotto, a Graduate and Dean of Villa Schifanoia in Florence Italy, received permission to open the self-sustaining program with a mission of nurturing artists in the growth and development of their creative expression. Doing this in New Mexico was of particular interest to Sister Giotto due to the spirit of the Native American and Hispanic cultural influences that are present here. She believed those influences were congruent with those of the artist. Within the campus was Joseph's Table, an income producing, student-staffed dining hall, an Art Gallery which displayed the work of the students, two story residential studios, accommodating up to 12 students at a time, and the chapel, Capilla de Nuestra Señora de Guadalupe, dedicated to Our Lady of Guadalupe. Within the Chapel, a shrine is built in her honor. While Catholic in concept, the Sagrada was intended to welcome all non-Catholic and non-Christian artists. Today, the Chapel is a sacred public place in

Albuquerque's Old Town providing comfort to those seeking a sanctuary for quiet prayer and meditation.

However, this location is not without its permanent residents. A mysterious figure has often been seen seated in the chapel, weeping profusely for some unknown tragic loss. The ghost is dressed in a long black dress, her face concealed by a dark veil. She is often mistaken for a real person, and sometimes ignored, until she mysteriously vanishes. This stop on the Ghost Tour of Old Town doesn't hold up when placed under the scrutiny of a scientific investigation.

OLD HONEYWELL BUILDING
BLUEWATER
ALBUQUERQUE, NEW MEXICO

Figure 43: Old Honeywell Building

There is not a lot of information about the old Honeywell Building on Bluewater. However, legend says that this building was built over an old Native American grave and if so, this could explain a lot. It is reported that a young woman will appear in the supply area. She is said to simply walk through the closed door and simply stare at the workers. Others have reported that she has been seen in the IT section at the other end of the building.

INDEX

www.ingramcontent.com/pod-product-compliance
Lightning Source LLC
Chambersburg PA
CBHW060804210726

48292CB00013B/1752